Rescue From Ithral

D.K. Webber

DEDICATION

To my best friend and husband Mr Webber.
Thank you so much for being my biggest supporter.
You are awesome and I could not have done this without
you. Thank you for taking care of me, encouraging me and
being proud of me the whole way through writing, editing,
and publishing.

CONTENTS

ACKNOWLEDGMENTS

Many thanks to Ellie, Megan, Hannah, Sarah, Shem, and Jethro who have also helped and supported me in this writing journey through discussions, proofreading, suggestions, and brainstorming.

AUTHORS NOTE

This story was started based on a dream I had in October 2020, and it has since developed and grown into what it is now, filled with raw emotion and many reflections of real pain and growth.

Chapter 1

Crash

Smoke filled the air from the explosions of ships and fighters that had crashed and now erupted in the distance.

I painfully pulled myself out of the wreckage of several crashed fighters and looked around me dazed. Moments before, an EMP blast had left vehicles, ships and weapons of both Elites and Reacher's totally useless. They had started shutting down and dropping from the sky like dead flies. I knew it wasn't my team or the enemies for that matter, neither would risk their own people's lives with something as reckless as this. Yet someone had set it off.

Agonizingly I got my left leg free from the twisted metal and groaned when I saw the bleeding tear running up my flight pants, from my ankle to my thigh. I grimaced and dragged myself towards the shelter of a nearby cliff.

Breathlessly I pulled myself up sitting against the rock face, clenching my teeth hard to stop from screaming in pain. With the movement I could feel that at least two ribs were in the wrong place.

I gingerly pressed a hand to my left side against my lower ribs and felt another gash that was bleeding steadily. At the same time, I felt blood running down the left side of my face from a cut just above my eyebrow. Un-clipping my battered helmet I pulled it off and breathed more freely, though it still felt somewhat difficult. I sat there panting against the rocks wondering how I had survived and how long it would take to bleed out.

Voices startled me, they came from around the corner and were getting closer. Now I could hear at least three distinguishably and they were most definitely the enemy. Turning I scrambled to pull myself up onto my feet with aid from the rocks. The instant I put weight on my left leg I collapsed and almost shrieked in pain. Rolling onto my right side I clamped a hand to my mouth to smother any noise and the other to my left side to stay the bleeding.

I saw them come around the rocky corner, three Reacher soldiers with guns at the ready. On seeing me the middle one's face flashed in pity and pain but the other two went rigid, ready to fire, their faces flashed with anger and hatred.

"Hold it you two!" the middle one shouldered his gun "Can't you see she's incapacitated?" coming forward he knelt beside me.

I snapped my eyes shut ready for the bullet or stab that would inevitably end my life, but it didn't come, and I opened them again. The other two held their ground, guns still at the ready.

"Stan, get back!" the tall one called angrily "She's Elite"

"I can see that," Stan answered casually, inspecting my torn leg.

"Stupid doctors," the second one muttered.

I heard that clearly, if this man was a doctor, it didn't matter who's side *I* was on, he would want to help me. That was only if he was a *true* doctor, if not he'd be as likely to kill me himself as let the others do it. But he hadn't yet so there was hope.

My eyes brimmed with pained tears as I watched him in despairing hope. He looked back, meeting my gaze with a calm and softening expression.

"I am going to help you"

"Freaking hell Stan! You can't be serious!" It was the tall one again and he was much angrier than before. Stan turned

"I am dead serious Marc! You two can go on without me if you wish but I am going to help *save* life no matter whose life it is" he turned back to me and pulled a large bag off his shoulder.

The other two glared at me menacingly but lowered their guns on seeing their friend's resolve.

"There's not much you can do anyway; you don't have the right equipment and she's as good as dead in this condition"

The doctor frowned as he hurriedly pulled supplies out of his bag "That's helpful Hank" he muttered "But I try not to underestimate myself or my patients, it's a bad idea! And, we also have no way of contacting or getting back to HQ!

That EMP knocked out and fried everything, everything! So, effectively, we are stranded here till help comes to us"

I saw the other two flinch at these matter-of-fact statements.

And seeing as this is the only other survivor we have come across apart from ourselves, I'd say there's a low chance many others survived"

The air was split by the noise of fresh explosions as several fighters of a reconnaissance squadron lost control and crashed several kilometres away.

I wondered if another EMP had gone off then remembered the final readings of my fighter's computer and gasped out "CEMP"

"What's that?" asked Marc still looking in the direction of the most recent crash and fumbling his dead wristband.

"Continuous Electromagnetic Pulse" Stan interpreted slowly with a sad sigh "Help isn't coming anytime soon, that EMP field is still up and anything that flies into it will get fried"

"Great, just freaking great," mumbled Hank "Stuck in this junk yard for who knows how long with unknown hostiles everywhere and probably natives trying to kill or eat us too"

"And nothing we can do about it!" Marc said in cold rage punching the rock wall.

I instinctively shuddered with fear at his display of raw anger.

"No, nothing at all" Stan confirmed "But you could go look for survival supplies, flexible wires or any soft padding in that fighter's wreckage"

"No way am I helping that Elite" Marc snorted furiously.

"I didn't ask you to help her" Stan retorted "I asked you to get *us* those supplies!"

Hank huffed but went off towards the nearest wreckage followed by a very angry Marc. Both must have realized that I was right about the CEMP. The electromagnetic pulse was still up as some kind of field, preventing any mobilized assistance.

Stan turned back to me and reached for my side. I rolled away from him onto my back and instantly closed my eyes as the ripple of pain shot through my entire body, threatening to vocalize.

"Easy, easy there" he said quietly "I don't want to hurt you, I just need to see the extent of your injuries, try not to move" Once more he reached to move my hand "May I...please?"

Was he asking for permission to touch me. But I was basically dead anyway? Holding the hand over my mouth tighter I let my side go in answer. He inspected the gash, and I could feel his fingers against my rib cage, surprisingly gentle. But I reeled in pain when he reached the broken ones.

"Sorry" he said softly "I don't have much with me, so this is going to hurt like hell"

I looked at him with fresh agony in my eyes, silently begging him to finish me off. He looked grim knowing what I was asking but seemed to dismiss it. My face twisted and I convulsed; he slightly lifted and turned me over pulling my hand away from my mouth as I coughed up blood.

"Not good" he muttered "Internal bleeding from those ribs and, I'm afraid there's a collapsed lung"

Gently he lowered me back to the ground as I gasped for air through the pain.

"You are one piece of work I tell you" he tried to smile as he washed the wounds and bandaged me up as best he could with his emergency kit.

Thankfully the leg tear wasn't very deep, and it didn't take many resources to stop the bleeding from my side and head. But my breathing didn't become much easier.

"I'll stitch you up later when we are in a better position, I hope that isn't long"

I shuddered as he gave me an injection.

"This is some pain reliever, it's going to hurt more moving you than it did bandaging you up, I've saved most of it for when I suture"

I swallowed and tried to say thank you.

"Shhh" he shook his head "Don't talk it won't help your lungs"

Marc and Hank came back at this moment carrying several supply bags and an armful of seemingly junk. Hank grudgingly tossed a fighter med kit to Stan who took it gratefully.

"The good news is we found a cave further down the cliff" Marc said pointing in the direction they had come "Plus there are some cargo crates nearby, hopefully they have more rations,"

"And the bad news?" Stan raised an eyebrow as he packed up his bag.

Hank looked uneasy "Some sort of creatures running around, we didn't see them fully before they dashed off but from what we did see I'd say they were large felines"

Stan nodded "Can't have everything easy now, can we?"

Marc looked annoyed and gave me a distrusting glance "Nothing about this is *easy*"

Stan shouldered his bag "Come on, let's get to that cave before dusk" he hesitated for a moment, still kneeling next to me "May I?"

I was still confused wondering what he was asking for but nodded feebly, he leant forward and picked me up in his arms. The movement happened so fast I barely registered the crippling pain till it reached my head... then I gasped and fainted.

Chapter 2

Shelter

A flickering light glinted off the rock ceiling as I slowly opened my eyes. I was lying on my right side, my whole body felt dull, numb and stiff as well as somewhat bare. My mind became acutely aware of my lack of clothes and how I was only in my underwear, mostly covered by a light emergency blanket. I wondered why then felt a strange pulling feeling on my left side. I suddenly recalled that Stan must be stitching me up, that numb feeling was the anaesthetic.

But even now I could feel it slipping away. As it was, I could feel a dull throbbing pain in my left leg. I closed my eyes again and tried not to think about it. If I could just fall back asleep till it was all over. He had started, it would be best to finish it and if he knew I was awake he'd definitely stop. The anaesthetic kept wearing off steadily.

I fought every urge to twist and move or scream as I slowly began to feel more pain in my side. Every stab and pull of the needle and thread stung and the awful burning from the leg gash hurt terribly. The pain tore at my mind, yet I somehow held it all in, there was no need to make any sound or move. I knew I could do this, I knew I had the self-control, but it was still hard.

My stomach churned with a sick feeling from the pain, but I didn't move. Slowly it felt like the pain was so great it no longer had an effect, my mind was numb, and I felt strangely calm. Perhaps it was shock? I was still and silent ever and to an onlooker it would seem as if I were still unconscious.

Stan, doctor though he was, must have been too focused on his work, now stitching up my forehead, to pick up on any change I had made upon becoming awake. I could feel the tight stiffness in my left leg, side and now forehead from the stitches and it made me want to stretch and pull against the sensation.

It seemed like he was finished as he cleaned up and re-bandaged the leg and side wounds. Pulling on what was left of my flight pants and jacket he gently rolled me onto my back before removing a needle that had been in my arm. I breathed a little more freely, the pain wasn't as intense now that I was still and he was no longer sewing.

Slowly my eyes drifted open, now freed from the mental strain I'd had on keeping them shut without making it noticeable. My whole body relaxed as I stared up at the dim ceiling. It was rugged rock and dark with shadows cast by the fire that must be in the cave entrance. I looked around without moving my head and saw Stan knelt next to me working on something in his bag.

He leant forward towards my feet and pulled the blanket up over me again. Then his eyes met mine before I could close them.

"Hello there" he smiled faintly as he gently applied a bandage to my forehead "How long have you been awake for?"

Unconsciously my glance snapped away from him to the wall, what could I say? I swore at myself, it was too late now to say that I had only just woken up, he wouldn't believe me. I could feel him watching me critically.

"What did you feel?" his voice was slightly strained.

I opened my mouth then shut it again, I couldn't bring myself to admit it and I was still in a lot of pain. Nor could I bring myself to look at him just now.

"Oh crap" he breathed sharply "You felt it all didn't you?"

Now I looked back at him, he'd dropped his face into his hands "I should have given you the whole dose in case you came to earlier, but I didn't and now for all I know you were awake the entire time I was working on you, and I hadn't even gotten your permission because you were unconscious"

I opened my dry mouth but still couldn't find any words. He looked down at my ghostly pale face, his flinching.

"I'm sorry," He whispered.

Now I found the words "You, you'd started" I gasped from the pain that talking caused my side "It was best for you to finish"

He stared in shock "What *did* you feel?"

I swallowed, I could see he honestly needed the truth "The side and head" I managed huskily.

"How did you do it?" he grimaced in disbelief.

"I...I don't know" I whispered "But thank you...for.... saving me"

He raised his eyebrows "Don't thank me yet, you're not nearly saved"

"How?" I swallowed.

He shook his head slowly "You have three fractured ribs, internal bleeding, a partially collapsed lung, a torn left leg, a gashed open side as well as the slash on your head, plus you're recovering from a concussion and desperately needed a blood transfusion"

A sighing breath left my mouth shakily as I struggled not to move. I was no doctor, but my imagination was good enough to recognize that I was seriously in danger.

"W-wait" I stuttered "Needed? b-blood transfusion?"

He nodded.

"But how? You have n-no blood to give me?"

"Well," he paused for a moment as he moved a few instruments next to me "By some miracle Hanks and my blood type are compatible with yours, Hanks would have been better, but I couldn't risk asking him and letting them know what I was going to do"

I was bewildered. "You g-gave me your blood? But-"

He smiled "Don't worry I'll be fine; it was enough to save you and not harm me"

If I wasn't overwhelmed before I sure was now, he had given me his own blood? We weren't even in a hospital, how had he managed without the proper equipment? Suddenly

I didn't want to know, the thought churned my stomach again.

He moved to my left side and seemed to be working on something. Whatever it was I could feel it moving in the side of my chest.

"What....what is that?" I asked through clenched teeth almost fearfully as I stared hard at the ceiling.

His answer was quiet but steady. "It's a three-way stopcock inserted into your chest cavity to remove the extra air"

I felt the panic building. No, no I had to stop it; I didn't want to move.

He recognized the changed pace of my breathing and gripped my hand. "You're going to be fine, calm your breathing, hyperventilating or panicking won't help anyone least of all you"

It took a few moments to get myself back under control. Gently he raised my head and gave me a drink from a canteen.

"I don't know your name, may I?" he asked curiously.

"Winta Yovacar" I replied, half absent mindedly as I looked around more and wondered why he hadn't just read my dog tag.

I was lying near the back of a large cave that was illuminated by the light of a fire at its entrance. Hank and Marc sat on either side of it working on their weapons, I assumed they were cleaning their guns.

Stan noticed my curious observations and he lowered me back down "We've decided to stay the night here, the men found some good survival resources and equipment in the supply crates, hungry?"

I blinked blankly at his question, still unable to process that he was a Reacher helping me, an Elite. Marc snorted and I glanced over catching his furious glare before he stalked out of the cave into the gathering darkness. I swallowed and found it hard, well at least one of these men wanted to kill me.

Stan was frowning after watching Marc leave, he shook his head and turned back to a crate "He'll come around I'm sure" he muttered "Just gone to blow off some steam, he still believes it was the Elites that set this CEMP off"

I felt anger twist my pained face "That's absurd! We'd never..."

His hand rested on my shoulder "Easy going, I know it wasn't you guys"

I tried to shake his hand off but ended up choking on a painful shriek, his hand held tighter on my shoulder.

"Don't move, it'll hurt more! you need to stay still"

I heard a sharpness in his tone I hadn't picked up before, was he ordering me? He was a doctor, of course he was. My eyes snapped shut and my fists unconsciously clenched, everything was so wrong! I shouldn't be alive let alone in the custody of Reacher's.

I wanted to scream out all the pain and anger, but I couldn't with my lungs this damaged, so I fought to block everything out. To ignore my senses and nerves and try to will myself to sleep through the usual military training steps. Relaxing and breathing while letting my mind clear, on an ordinary day I could do it in sixty seconds. But I'd never tried to do it while in so much pain before, and now I found it impossible. This scenario hadn't exactly been covered in my academy training.

It may have been minutes; it may have been hours by the time I finally gave up. Opening my eyes I saw that the light had grown much dimmer, two dark silhouettes sat by the fire, but I couldn't see a third. Has Marc not returned yet?

A sharp and drawn-out feline scream pierced the silence. Both silhouettes leapt to their feet grabbing their guns as they did. I felt my body try to force itself to action, but I struggled to lie still. The ground shook slightly as the sound of a nearby explosion followed the scream. A moment later Marc dashed through the cave entrance and skidded to a stop on this side of the fire.

"Wood on the fire Quick!!" he called, grabbing a handful from the pile they had gathered and tossed it into the blaze.

The other two helped him and soon the fire roared hot and bright with flames almost reaching the ceiling. On the other side of the flames at the entrance of the cave snarls and shrieks started.

"What in the blazers are those?" Hank asked.

Marc laughed "Those are the biggest cats you'll ever see, darn it they almost had me at one point" he laughed again as if he enjoyed the memory and fired a bullet from his rifle into the darkness, he smiled in satisfaction hearing a pained screech. A few moments later silence fell once more.

"Sounds like they've left now" Stan said, locking and putting down the gun he'd grabbed. "I'd say they're mostly nocturnal, so they'll stay around all night, best we keep this fire going to keep them at bay"

Marc scoffed "They'll be looking for shelter elsewhere, I spotted a storm coming up from the west"

With some annoyance I wondered how long we'd be stuck here as I felt my eyes close. I didn't fight the exhaustion and a moment later drifted off to sleep to the crackle of fire.

Chapter 3

Storm

I was cold then I was hot. Shivering and sweaty, trapped in a restless sleep taunted by pain. Darkness tried to hold together but soon it slipped away and my eyes opened staring at a cold stone roof. I listened to the clap of thunder and the downpour of rain from the storm that raged outside as memories returned, recalling the past few days to my mind.

The mission briefing as the carrier ships sped through hyperspace towards. Ithral. Squad five's commander had assigned me as his wing man. The argument about the chosen battle point. Heading to the fighter bays. My squadron's huddled debrief before strapping into our individual speed fighters.

My squad's mission was to protect the two bombers we'd been assigned; they needed to get through and hit the

Reacher's base. I saluted through the cockpit. The carriers dropped out. Bombers and fighters launched. We cleared the atmosphere and started our approach in perfect formations. Sensors picked up the enemy fighters inbound. The air battle had ensued with ferocity. One of my squad had gone down. I shot down two Reacher's.

Suddenly out of nowhere an explosion erupted from a nearby mountain range, an energy wave seemed to balloon out heading right for us. I had watched in helpless horror as fighter after fighter had dropped from the sky as the pulse enveloped them. Then my fighter lost all power as the energy wave overtook me. My ejection mechanism was fried, and I had no choice but to ride my lifeless ship down.

As I plummeted towards the ground, I saw my squad commander's fighter engulfed in a ball of fire ahead of me. Then another powerless craft smashed into mine. My helmet hit the control panel, and I knew no more until I awoke with my leg caught in the twisted metal to the sounds of explosions.

Jolted back to reality I struggled to pull myself along until somewhat propped up with my back against the cave wall. Whatever was in my side had been strapped on by the bandages tight around my torso supporting my broken ribs. Still, it hurt savagely, and I was left breathing hard as I pulled the blankets back over my legs.

Looking around I saw Stan fast asleep sitting half hunched up against the opposite wall. Over at the entrance a figure stood up and started walking towards me, I recognized it as Marc. Our eyes met then mine glanced at the rifle beside Stan's unconscious form.

The snap second thought flashed through my mind, "*I could make it there before he did*". As soon as it came it was replaced by a realistic view, there was no way I would make it there without keeling over from the pain. And Marc could easily shoot me first; it sure looked like he wanted to. The frown on his face had changed to a menacing scowl when he had noticed my glance at the gun.

Kneeling in front of me he smirked "You're only alive because my idiot friend here happens to be a doctor!!"

I glanced from him to Stan then back again "I'm aware" I failed to keep my voice from shaking.

He chuckled upon seeing the contraption attached to my side and I gasped with pain as he touched a pipe curiously.

"Well, I wonder if this is vital in keeping you alive, guess I should have paid more attention in first aid class"

I gritted my teeth and turned my head away feeling the anger building up from my helpless state.

"Oh, I'm sorry, did that hurt?" he leant slightly closer, chuckling in amusement. Putting his hand under my chin he turned my face back to face him. I locked my jaw as our eyes met again.

"Listen carefully Elite, I won't hesitate to shoot you the instant you try anything! Understood?"

I feebly nodded, I supposed it was only fair.

"Good," he dropped my chin. "Though I suppose a slow death is more fitting after that EMP you cowards set off".

Standing up he walked back towards the entrance as I bit my lip hard, stopping myself from responding. I noticed it was only us three in the cave and wondered where Hank was. Almost as if in answer to my thoughts he appeared dripping wet at the entrance of the cave. Taking off his raincoat he tossed a couple of bags and cases to one side.

"This is all I could find amongst the second closest wreckage, looked like the cats had been cleaning up the dead before the storm hit"

I shuddered as the involuntary thought of *"or almost dead"* flashed through my mind and how very nearly that had been me.

Hank hung up his wet coat then sat down by a crate and pulled out an emergency food package. Another deafening clap of thunder seemed to shake the ground and Stan started awake. Standing up he stretched his stiff limbs and, seeing me awake he smiled. I looked away, unable to return it. How could anyone smile in a time like this? And under these circumstances?

I was almost sure it would be easier if he ignored me just like the others, but he simply would not. I knew Mark and Hank blamed Elites for the EMP, and I wondered why Stan didn't.

Sitting down beside me he offered an emergency ration pack. I had half a mind to decline it, but my hunger was real, so I humbly accepted it. Eating was hard but I refused to show just how bad it hurt.

"I need to check the wounds to see if all the stitches are secure and if there's any infection" he said, putting his now empty pack down.

I stopped mid chewing and glanced at him awkwardly.

He read my face and looked at his two friends then back to me, shrugging he sighed "Well I don't want it to get infected, if I can help it"

I managed to finish the ration pack, putting it down I sighed unconsciously trying to sit more comfortably.

"You okay?"

I looked up and nodded.

"Because I need to remove that stopcock and get you to walk so that the wounds heal properly"

I could feel whatever colour was left in my face drain away as I imagined limping around barely clothed in front of these three men. He looked so sympathetic, but I wasn't sure it helped much.

"Well..." he hesitated a little uncomfortably "I'll grab some blankets and my gear and set it up at the very back of the cave, then I'll help you over"

I guessed it must be easier to ask consent when the patient was unconscious.

He ferried a few cases and bags to the end of the cave, set up a thermal lamp, laid out a few emergency blankets and opened a couple of the cases. As he approached me, I found just how unprepared I was.

It only took the work of a moment to remove the stopcock and seal the hole; it stung horribly but I bore it knowing that worse was possibly coming.

"Okay if you put your right arm around my neck like this, I'll help you stand up"

It took more will than strength to trust him with my weight and then stand up. Putting any weight on my left leg hurt and all the stitches pulled tight with any movement, but I could stand. I'm pretty sure that if my face wasn't so deathly pale from pain and blood loss it would have turned bright red.

The other two men were now watching us, and I was acutely aware of just how dilapidated my clothes were. The left pants leg was almost ripped the entire way up to my waist while my fighter jacket was torn open on the left side.

With painful steps we made it to the end of the cave, and he lowered me down behind a few crates till I lay on my right side on the blankets. I wasn't looking forward to this at all, but my reason knew better and, foreign though it was, I trusted this Reacher.

"May I.... please?" he asked kindly.

I nodded and he half removed my jacket.

Thankfully my side wound wasn't infected though he did have to put two stitches in again. I gritted my teeth and kept my eyes shut; it was the best way to get through this.

Pulling a loose blanket over my re-bandaged torso he moved to the leg. To my relief he could access the whole limb through the rip. It too was not infected.... yet, and no stitches needed repairing.

Re-bandaging the leg he gently rolled me onto my back and pulled the blanket down, covering me completely. Then he unwound the head bandage. I felt the cold of a wet cloth as he cleaned it before the dreaded sting of a needle and the pull of string. As calm as I tried to stay, I found I didn't have the will, strength or control I had had last night. Consequently, the tears slipped down my cheeks and my breathing quickened.

"I'm sorry," he whispered.

At last, I felt him apply a fresh bandage, but I kept my eyes shut and teeth clenched, I didn't have control over myself yet and felt like bursting into sobs.

I sensed him leave and heard the movement of some of the crates. Voices rose into what sounded like an argument, but I couldn't distinguish what they said.

After what felt like ages the voices died down and I slowly opened my eyes feeling less like crying. The crates had been moved, shielding me even more from the rest of the cave. Slowly I pulled myself up sitting, with the blanket tight around me. Stan walked up holding a bundle in his hand.

His face was set in anger as he handed it to me "I'm sorry Winta, but this is the best I could do"

I took it with a shaking hand though I could see he wasn't angry at me. He turned and left, and I stared at the clothes in my hands, a Reacher jacket and pants. They looked like they might have been pulled out of an emergency survival kit, but I couldn't help thinking of the worst-case scenario. Shuddering, I tried not to think about it.

Shielded by the crates I took off my torn Elite clothes and put on the Reacher's uniform. I hated the feeling and very idea of wearing my enemies' colours, but I was grateful to be fully covered again. At some point I had been wearing a tank top, but I assumed Stan had had to remove whatever was left of it when originally stitching me up.

My breathing was still rather laboured from the strain on my weak lung but at least it was recovering. I winced as I struggled to my bare feet with the support of the wall, though the clothes fitted well enough they felt foreign and trapping.

Taking a long breath, I started walking beside the wall out into the main cave cavity. The three men were standing near the entrance seemingly deep in an earnest conversation. Hank looked up and, on seeing me, tapped Stan's shoulder. Stan turned, a flash of surprise taken by concern crossed his face before he dashed towards me.

"What are you doing?" he exclaimed.

Reaching me he wrapped my right arm around his neck while slipping his other arm around my waist. It was then that I realized how lightheaded and near falling over I was, though I wasn't sure exactly why.

He helped me back to where I had originally woken up and pulled a blanket around my shoulders.

"I know I said you need to walk but not without help next time, okay? You almost fainted!"

I didn't answer, he was right I had almost fainted, but I could only guess it was from shock, blood loss and stress.

The rest of the day passed uneventfully. I tried to sleep as much as I could while the storm continued and I began to feel dreadfully cold.

Upon waking up the next day I found I was very sick. It was still just as stormy as when I had fallen asleep. My sickness grew worse over the course of the day and the fever settled into restlessness and delirium. Stan was worried, fearing an internal infection yet couldn't be sure and he also had no more antibiotics left.

I was barely there most the afternoon, wandering in and out of consciousness. Sometimes muttering here and there, all the while not helping the growing restlessness of the three men.

Once I remember Stan bending over me anxiously, I couldn't remember why. Maybe I had woken up with a scream from a delirious nightmare? Who knows.

I don't remember that night much, apart from the faint clap of thunder and the steady crackling of the fire.

On the third day of the storm, I woke with a start and sat up only to gasp with the pain and fall back onto the blankets. In the dream I'd been falling after the EMP went off only this time I had been outside the cockpit free falling with no parachute.

I sighed then took a deep breath, it was hard on my lungs, but it was getting easier. A noise nearby made me snap around and swing my arm in a defensive move that I'd forgotten I owned. Stan was kneeling by my side; he'd caught my arm mid swing.

"Easy going there Winta, please tell me you aren't still delirious"

I dropped my arm "I-I don't think so?"

He sighed in relief "You don't feel sick?"

I shook my head, I didn't feel overly cold or lightheaded.

"Any unusual pain anywhere?"

Again, I shook my head.

"That's good, I'm hoping it wasn't too serious an infection then"

The day seemed to drag on forever. Twice Stan aided me to walk around for a bit to help with the healing wounds. Both Hank and Marc just seemed to sit by the entrance in their dark Reacher coats as the storm raged on. The patience they seemed to have and the ominous brooding feeling that emanated from them was unsettling. I was almost going insane with my immobility and the pain as well as the feeling of being a hostage.

When the night finally came, I fought the nagging urge to kill them all and escape free. I don't know how it came but the feeling was so intense. I could just grab that gun and shoot all three of them even if Marc was waiting. I'd shoot him first!

But I owed them my life. Even if Stan was the one who had saved me the other two *had* shown me mercy instead of killing me instantly, they'd spared my life. If I killed them right now it would be in cold blood, treacherous and dishonourable

I dismissed the thought and willed myself to sleep, grateful to be alive however long they let me live.

Chapter 4

Embark

"At least I wasn't insane yet" was my thought on waking up on the fifth day. The instant I looked around I noticed the quiet. No wind, no rain, no thunder. The storm had passed, and sunlight shone dimly through the cave's entrance.

I felt my heart jump, I could leave this place, perhaps find others and return to Elita.

The next second reality struck me; there was no leaving. I was their prisoner; a captive held for interrogation or maybe even ransom. I looked up again. The three men were loading the survival essentials into their packs. I felt myself backing up against the wall and pulling my knees up under my chin. What was going to happen to me?

Finally, when everything was ready, packs shouldered and guns in hand, Stan came over to me. He gestured my Elite boots towards me, offering to put them on. I met his eyes and nodded slightly. After clipping them on he offered me his hand. I didn't want to take it, but I accepted the help. Standing gingerly on my feet I wondered if I would faint again, but the dizziness passed, and I found I was alright.

Heading towards the cave entrance following behind the others I leant on Stan's shoulder to take some weight off my leg. Besides, I was too self-conscious to shrug him off.

As I emerged from the entrance and stepped into the sunlight I was met with Marc's menacing scowl. He held a pair of cuffs, and I knew exactly what was coming. Stan went stiff and I sensed him growing angry. Hank handled his rifle uneasily as Marc advanced.

"She might be your patched up patient Stan but, while we are on the move, she's, *my* prisoner!"

His harsh tone sent a shiver down my spine and the word prisoner drained the remaining colour from my face. I gave no protests as he clipped my hands together in front of me and, for all our sake, I hoped Stan would not protest. We were not the same, but he was a doctor who had the blessing of being able to see all of us as equals. I saw Marc as a merciless Reacher. Marc saw me as a ruthless Elite. Stan saw both of us as human beings wanting to live.

"Marc, you are a coward!!"

I gulped hearing Stan's steady but furious voice. Marc was still glaring down at me, but I saw his face cloud over in rage that made me shrink back in fear. He spun around to face the doctor, and Hank held my arm restrained. He must have thought I might engage, but he was wrong; there was no way I was going near those two.

"I am not a coward!" Marc said, towering over Stan who still didn't seem daunted in the slightest.

"You are!" Stan replied, "Because you are afraid of her while she poses no threat! Even a crate trader could see it"

Marc's unsteady voice portrayed his fury as he struggled to not punch the shorter man.

"I am not putting up with this, she is still Elite no matter how 'hurt' or 'helpless' she might seem! I am the commanding officer here so be grateful I haven't shot her yet. Now, stand down, that's an order!"

There was another moment of heavy tension before Stan, who seemed to be calculating the safest outcomes, conceded and turned away. He was still outraged but had evidently decided this was the best choice. The next moment Marc was walking off and Hank guided me along while Stan brought up the rear.

As we walked it seemed like the tension slowly faded and, after what felt like about an hour, Stan was walking next to Marc discussing survival plans.

"We'll continue west and hope to make it out of the fields range" Marc was saying "Should be able to get a drop ship pick up then" he said glancing at Stan and answered his unasked question "Yes we will collect any survivors we come across along the way"

I processed what they were saying. Were they just going to walk out of here? But the field was still up, and rescue ships were not able to get in? Marc had guessed this, but I wondered if he'd thought about the outside not knowing about the field. More lives could be lost if it stayed up, not just from lack of rescuing but perhaps the very rescuers themselves. For all I knew rescue ships had already been lost while trying to land during the storm.

"What?!" I exclaimed and both men turned around, my mind was racing with ideas and plans "We can't just walk out of here!"

Marc scowled "Of course we can!"

"But-but the field is still up!!" I was thinking hard for a way to shut it down.

Marc looked around "So? It won't stop us walking out"

I looked at Stan and could see he had started thinking along the same line as me.

"She's right" he said slowly, Marc glared at him.

I blurted out "No rescue ships can get *here* to pick up the other survivors! *We* have to shut it down"

Now Marc was bristling again, he stormed over to me "And I suppose you know how to do that?!"

I was shaking a little "Yes, I-I'm a tech engineer".

He nodded his head angrily "Oh perfect just what I thought, and I suppose you know where the generator is?"

I opened my mouth but fell short of words. He was accusing me of setting the EMP off, wasn't he? My face grew red in anger and Stan put his hand on Marc's shoulder trying to pull him away.

"Marc, stop it! She doesn't know where it is"

Marc flung Stan's hand off his shoulder "Answer me!! Where is the generator?"

I cowered back even though I was still angry "Elites didn't do this!!"

He smirked seemingly enjoying my anger "Oh and of course Elites can be trusted"

"I could say the same for Reacher's!" I bit back.

"No, you can't!! Because you attacked us!!"

Stan had given up and stepped away and it was now a good thing Hank was holding me back.

"Reacharva had no claim on this moon!! It's under Elita jurisdiction!"

Marc scoffed "Jurisdiction! It's not under the Elita claim code! Reacharva had every right to mine here!"

I was furious "You know that's a lie!!"

Marc just laughed "Well if Ithral is under Elita's claim then where is this EMP generator?!"

I blinked blankly; he'd brought it right back around.

"I-I don't know... it's not Elite so I don't know"

Marc nodded "Fine then, you don't know where it is so we can't shut it down! So, we walk out and get a pickup!" He turned to walk off as if in victory.

"We have to try and find it!" I quickly added, hopeless that he would listen when I was startled by Hank's voice.

"She's right"

Marc glanced at him with a surprise that quickly dissolved into anger again.

"Surviving Reacher's can't get rescued from here if the ships can't get in" Hank added thoughtfully "And there may be many who can't just walk out like we could"

Marc went to say something but Stan, now emboldened by Hank speaking up, cut him off.

"Marc, they have a point, we have to try and look for the generator"

Marc was evidently boiling over again "Where the heck do you think it is? That field could be generated from anywhere. How are we supposed to find it?"

"One of the mountain ranges" I said hopefully, racking my memory back to the explosion I had seen "We have to try"

Marc seemed to shrug as though he no longer cared. I brightened up hoping he would at least not stop us from looking. Suddenly he spun around and knocked Hank away from me. Before I could react, his fist collided with the left side of my face, knocking me to the ground stunned.

I scrambled to my knees, breathing hard as my ear rang painfully and the cut above my eye felt numb. The cold iron of a rifle barrel pressed hard against the back of my head, and I froze. I saw Stan and Hanks shocked faces, barely able to believe their commander's action.

"Marc don't!" Stan cried in horror.

"She's right!" Hank said angrily.

Marc's rage felt thick behind me. "Since when did you guys start trusting Elites more than your own Reacher brothers?!!" he seethed "You know she is only trying to use us to bide time! How are you so blind?!"

I was shaking with uncontrollable fear knowing death was so close, all he needed to do was pull the trigger and I'd be gone forever. I didn't want to die!!! The prospect was terrifying, and I could barely keep myself from falling to the ground.

I heard Stan's reasoning voice strained with desperation "Marc it's not that at all, we don't trust her more than you, but there might be survivors and it's our responsibility to try to help them"

"Well," Marc said quietly, as though his initial rage had lost its edge, "Even if we do go looking for it, we sure as hell don't need her!"

The barrel pressed harder, and I caught my breath in a sharp gasp waiting for the bullet that would put a hole in my head. But it didn't come, for the next second a deep hum drew our attention to the northern sky. A Reacher cruiser had descended from the clouds most likely responding to a distress call now that the storm had cleared.

I felt the horrible realization of what was about to happen and breathed "Oh please no"

A shrill metallic yearning screech split the air as it passed through the field a few kilometres away and lost power. There was nothing we could do but watch on in helpless sadness. It plummeted to the ground with an explosion that erupted into a mushroom cloud.

The barrel left my skull, and I unconsciously relaxed letting out a shaky breath as I did. Stan was by my side in a moment and lifted me to my trembling feet. I saw Marc, his face was now set in dark sadness that was overshadowed by a solemn fury, no longer directed at me.

"Let's go find that freaking generator and blow it to hell" he growled before stalking away up the mountain side.

I walked after him with Stan's help and Hank followed behind. I was pretty sure one or two stitches in my forehead had broken from the punch, but it was still too numb to feel it. No! I was not going to faint!! I would not let myself! But I sure felt like it.

"Are you okay?" Stan asked quietly.

I nodded hesitantly, not trusting my voice. No!! No way in life was I *okay*... I nearly got a bullet through my head for goodness' sake!! This was why I'd signed up and trained as a strike pilot. I couldn't handle combat or fighting unless I distanced myself from it in the cockpit. I didn't have to admit it though, Stan could guess I wasn't actually okay.

The next few hours were a painstaking walk up towards the mountain top. Marc stayed well ahead without saying a word and Hank stayed well behind, also in silence. Stan helped me the entire way, only ever saying what was needed to aid the trek.

Wreckage was scattered here and there but no ships or fighters were left on the mountain side, they had all either burnt up or rolled down to the valley.

Finally, we reached the top. I leant against what was left of a tree and looked around at the breathtaking carnage. For kilometres and kilometres around in all directions the forest and plains had burnt patches. So many trees were broken, vehicle wreckage here and there and debris spread around everywhere. It was heartbreaking. The entire scene had a dull muggy atmosphere after being drenched by the three-day storm. Over to the north the decimated Reacher ship was still smoking.

I slumped against a rock and Stan left me to go talk to Marc. After a moment of rest, I limped tiredly around the rock till I had a better vantage point. What was I looking for? I did my best to remember back to that first day when I'd seen the explosion and energy burst. It had come from a mountain range; I could vaguely remember the direction and general look.

Scanning the surrounding mountain ranges I saw the part that looked strikingly familiar. As I continued looking, I found it was the only part that looked familiar to my memory. Besides I could see significant burnt damage to the hillside from where the explosion must have come from. That or it was unfinished cover work, perhaps the base had been under construction? I wondered who it belonged to and why they had set it off. I guessed the generator facility would be disguised inside the ground, but it needed external emitters, and they must be hidden by the trees on top.

I slid down the rock and sat on the ground. This was going to be a long-time walking. The range was at least four days' walk away and probably longer with me in this condition.

Stan came back over to me leaving Marc and Hank talking on the far outcropping.

"Are you all good?"

I nodded but winced when I tried to sit up more comfortably.

He frowned "You can be honest, where does it hurt?"

I sighed "My leg and side, I think a few stitches broke on my head, oh and my jaw hurts"

He nodded sympathetically "I'm sorry about Marc, I'll have a look at the stitches tonight if you'd like, when we set up camp. Marc spotted what looks to be an organized gathering of survivors down in the west plains, but we can't tell who they are, so we had best avoid them for the moment"

I nodded "We should start heading southwest, that's the direction of the field generator facility"

He looked confused.

I waved towards the mountain range "Left flank second lowest dip, the one with trees on top and burnt hillside, that's where I saw the energy burst originate from, even if it's only one emitter it should still stop the CEMP if we shut it down"

Stan was eyeing me oddly and I rolled my eyes "It's not Elite believe me I know! Well, that's if you still trust me..." I broke off bitterly, I had trusted him, and he had said he didn't trust me.

A surprised look crossed his face "I do trust you"

I looked away.

"If you're referring to what I said to Marc earlier that was just to ease him, believe me I know you could have killed me by now if you wanted to"

My glance flashed back to him a little guiltily. "I'm sorry" I whispered, hardly believing what I just said. But it was still true, I was sorry I'd snapped at him, and I knew he hadn't actually said he didn't trust me.

"Don't be, I understand"

He helped me to my feet; this time I managed to nicely shrug him off and found I could walk by myself with minimal pain.

We approached the other two "Marc?" they both turned "Winta believes she found where the facility is"

Marc's eyes scowled at me menacingly, I guessed he was assuming I knew because it was an Elite base.

"Where?"

Stan nodded towards the mountains "Southwest, lower end of the mountain range to our best knowledge"

Marc looked at it for a while before turning back "Let's get started then"

He walked towards me, eyes fixed on mine, as he passed Stan, I heard him say "If she can't keep up, I'll shoot her" before stalking past me and down the way we'd come.

I'm not sure what my face looked like, but I believe it must have been a mix of terror and dread.

Stan sighed before walking over "Just ignore him Winta, he's just hot headed and annoyed at the moment, it'll blow over"

I turned and started down the mountain side which was not made easier by my cuffed hands. Would it just blow over though? Stan hadn't been the one with a gun to his head, I shuddered at the memory I was going to struggle to forget.

Chapter 5

Loss

In the woods we found it was cooler and fresher than the mountain side. Though it was dark and a bit damp I felt better out of the intense sun and open surroundings.

We didn't stop walking for several hours. Marc adjusted our course when we came out into a clearing and I liked to think that he believed me, but I was sure it was because Stan had said where the facility was and not me.

Of course, I wasn't sure that range was where the generator was, but it was the best guess any of us had. I didn't know what would happen to me if it turned out to be a false lead, so I tried not to think of it.

Despite all my fears I still managed to keep up with everyone else. Perhaps it was the will to live or the fear of death. I couldn't tell either way.

As we travelled along, we passed the wreckage of a few crashed ships. There were no bodies, much to my relief, but we did pick up a few more emergency food packs.

I couldn't keep an accurate track of time and didn't really try. It was too hard under the cover of the trees, but I could at least tell it was late afternoon.

Finally, as the light began to fade rapidly, we came to a stop at the base of a hill where the forest was extremely thick. Marc said this would do for the night and Hank set about lighting a fire and prepping some food packs. Most of the wood around was damp but there were several fallen trees that provided enough dry wood for a good fire.

I slumped down with my back against a tree trunk. It was now that I realized just how exhausted I truly was. How stiff and sore my limbs were and how laboured my breathing had become with a cough every now and again.

Stan brought over a pack of emergency food that had been heated up. I took it gratefully but avoided eye contact, it didn't help that I could feel his worried gaze turn to me every time my breath caught, or I coughed.

"Much pain?" he asked, inspecting my forehead wound.

I shook my head "It's-it's not bad, just my ribs and lungs are tired"

He sat down, a tree away "A couple of stitches are broken but I believe it's sealed well enough"

I was relieved as I didn't really want to have stitches put back in. We concentrated on eating for the next few minutes, and I wished Marc would take off my cuffs, but he showed no interest, and I was too afraid to ask.

Finishing my food, I put the empty pack down and stretched my leg. It was stiff and hurt but I tried not to show it. Stan wasn't fooled though, but there wasn't much he could do other than give me a blanket. He valued my life too much to push Marc again on the point of the cuffs, so I lay down under the blanket with my hands still restrained.

He was going to have the second watch, so he sat down near me with another survival blanket. I was just thinking how uncomfortable these cuffs would be to sleep in when Marc came over. Naturally I was scared but then I felt a little hopeful that he would free my hands for the night.

However, that hope was dashed when he attached a cable to the cuff and then wrapped it around the tree, I was next to before walking off muttering "If you can be trusted this won't be a problem"

I curled up miserably under the blanket and almost wished he'd just shoot me rather than treat me like this.

"I'm sorry Winta"

I looked up and saw Stan had shifted closer, he looked pitiably sad.

I frowned in annoyance. "What the heck do you care! I'm just an Elite so you might as well ignore me like your friends!"

Stan looked hurt and glanced over at his two companions on the far side of the clearing.

"I'm just a Reacher, why didn't you shoot me when you had the chance?"

I opened my mouth but closed it when his curious eyes met mine.

"Because you were nice to me" I whispered honestly as I pulled my head back under the blanket.

Even so I did wish he'd leave me alone, he was nice, and I didn't hate him like I did the other two, Hank less so than Marc. But I felt that he wasn't helping me anymore, it was ridiculous, but I was slowly getting angry at him again.

Even though he had said he trusted me, and I had felt relieved for a while it was now wearing off.

"What's Elita like?"

I looked up again this time in bewilderment "What?"

He smiled faintly as if he was trying to cheer me up with a change of subject "I was just wondering what your planet is like; I've never been there and Reacharva is rather boring being so populated"

I rested my head down on my arm "Elita is nice, it's not too built over as there are laws governing building to greenery ratios, it has the most beautiful forests, mountains and beaches and..." I paused as an overwhelming homesickness flooded over me, and I choked on a sob as tears filled my eyes.

Stan looked down at me in surprise before understanding flashed across his face.

"Winta I'm sorry I shouldn't have brought it up. I was just curious but... oh I'm so sorry"

He seemed to be going to slide closer to me, but I coiled away curling up tighter.

"Just leave me alone!!" I said huskily, fighting against emotion.

I was now really angry at him. I felt he had been so mean, perhaps he hadn't meant it but still. Deep down he was a

Reacher, and I wondered if he could be as cruel, cold and malicious as the others. I felt utter hopelessness enveloped me as I silently cried myself to sleep.

Waking up I felt exhausted, as if I hadn't slept for a moment. Stiffly I pulled myself up sitting and leant back against the tree looking around.

Marc was brooding by the smouldering fire and re-assembling his rifle and Stan sat over by the backpacks, re-packing them. Sharply my head snapped away from him as all the memories of last night flooded back.

I sighed and rubbed my grubby face brushing the scraggly brown hair away from my eyes. There were still at least three days to walk to the facility and my hopes of surviving them were slowly growing dimmer.

Suddenly an ear-splitting scream sounded not that far away. Marc and Stan jumped to their feet, and I cowered back against the tree that I was still attached to.

"Damn Cats!!" Marc spat "Hanks still out scouting"

He grabbed up his pack, slipped his arms through the straps then clipped it around his chest. Stan had done the same and held Hank's pack in his free hand. Where was Hank?

Marc tossed something that Stan caught "Get the prisoner"

Stan dashed to my side, un-clipped the cable and stuffed it into Hank's bag. I caught my breath painfully as he pulled me to my feet too fast and my head felt sickeningly fuzzy for a moment.

Marc held his rifle at the ready aimed at the far ridge.

"Come on Hank come on" he breathed.

The next few minutes felt horrible as we all waited anxiously for something to happen. Stan stood in front of me with his rifle to his shoulder and I could feel my terrified heart pounding.

Suddenly, bursting out of the bushes on the far ridge Hank came running at full speed and, right behind him, the biggest cat I had ever seen.

He saw us and threw himself to the side with a shout "MARC NOW!!" as he slid across the ground.

Marc's rifle echoed through the clearing as a bullet shot clear through the cat's eye, and it crashed to the ground with a deathly growl barely a meter behind Hank. He had leapt up again still at a run and then, skidding to a stop on his knees next to Stan, grabbed up his pack and clipped it on.

"Report!" Marc yelled.

Hank puffed breathlessly "A whole pack of about eleven cats are coming.... I'm guessing they're not nocturnal after all!!.... I couldn't find any clear way through the thick forest west...so we have to go more south"

"Come on!" Marc called and we all turned and followed him into the trees.

I could feel the panic surging through my veins as the sharp catcalls screeched closer then further away for another one to sound right on the other side of the trees we passed.

Suddenly, we came to a halt as three cats blocked our path snarling viciously. The men started firing and two fell instantly but the third dodged back into the trees.

"Damn it they're all around, back up" Hank called too late as two cats broke from the trees on our left and Marc couldn't react fast enough. I saw him thrown to the side by the cat's huge paw before Hank shot it down.

The second one was coming right for me when Stan's bullets almost severed one of its legs and left bleeding holes in the side of its skull. I was just in time to throw myself to the side before its body crashed to the ground right where I had been, lifeless.

I scrambled to my feet with too much adrenaline to register the pain while Hank helped Marc to his. The commander was okay but a bit winded.

"Come on let's go" Stan called, grabbing my arm and pulling me along after him.

The screech tore through the air, and I saw the cat launch before the others did. Without thinking I yanked Stan's rifle arm around and pulled the trigger. The bullet hit the cat square in its throat causing it to gurgle on its snarls and crash into a tree.

Another cat scream made me throw myself hard at Stan, knocking him to the ground. My head hit the earth hard, and I was disoriented. I heard yells and gun fire as I tried to clear my blurry vision, a deafening explosion knocked me to the right against a rock and left my ears ringing.

Then there was silence as my vision was restored, and the smoke and dust cleared. Fighting the cuffs I clamped a hand to my throbbing forehead as I staggered to my feet coughing and looked around.

Six cats' bodies lay around the place, three of them were seared and burning on the edge of a small crater where a grenade had gone off. I coughed and winced in pain then caught sight of Marc standing beside Stan.

I staggered over. Stan was bending over Hank as Marc stood by with his rifle at the ready. With a gasp I fell to my knees, Hank's neck and chest were ripped open and I could see there was no hope for him. Turning away as nausea almost made me vomit, I closed my eyes tight trying to banish the repulsive image. Clamping a hand over an ear I felt like screaming from the pain as the adrenaline wore off. I wasn't sure how long I had my eyes closed for; it may have been minutes or hours for all I knew.

A rough hand grabbed my arm and pulled me to my shaky feet; it was a stone-faced Marc. Glancing over I saw Stan piling dirt on where I assumed Hank was buried. The doctor hardly looked awake, pale faced with automatic movements, and I felt awfully sorry for him.

"Let's keep moving before the last two of those cursed things come back!!" Marc growled and yanked me along after him.

Marc's grip didn't let go for what seemed like hours as we hurried along, or he stormed along while I stumbled and staggered trying to not fall over or verbalize my pain. Stan followed behind, rather distant and utterly silent.

Finally, we came to a halt at the top of a hill and his hand released me. I slumped to the ground in exhaustion; there was no way I could keep going like this. I felt spent and sick with aching muscles and sore wounds. I needed a break.

Stan caught up and dropped the bags before standing beside Marc and looking out over the scenery.

"It's barely midday" Marc muttered "We should be able to turn a little south now and continue on t-"

"We should have a break," Stan interrupted and glanced at me "Winta can't go on like this"

Marc glared at me dangerously. "That's a shame, tell me Elite, do you want a bullet or the cats?"

I grimaced at the idea of death by the cats and involuntarily retched before vomiting as the gruesome memory of Hank flashed through my mind. Marc's taunting laugh rang in my ears as I tried to breathe a bit easier and not throw up again.

"What a soldier," he chuckled in harsh amusement. "The sight of death and a bit of blood makes you sick? how pathetic"

"Shut up!" Stan yelled "She has every right to be sick! She's weak, exhausted, frightened from the cats, affected by Hank's death, then you force her to walk for hours in the heat and now you're threatening her with death!! Leave her be!!!"

I glanced up in surprise at Stan's outburst and saw a furious Marc stalking up to the doctor.

Stan shrugged "What are you going to do? Shoot me? Go ahead, I don't even care!!"

With that he pushed past the commander and handed me a water bottle. Marc threw down his pack and stormed off over the hill. It was good to clean out my mouth and have a fresh drink, but I was feeling horribly guilty for ever being angry with Stan. He was still kind to me even after losing his friend and falling out with his commander.

"I'm sorry Stan" I faintly managed to say.

He shook his head "I understand but.... I have to thank you for saving my life"

I didn't quite register what he said. I was fighting against tears that threatened to fall from the guilt I felt after misjudging him. As well as the haunting image of Hank's twisted pale face that kept coming into my mind and I couldn't shake it.

"Easy now" Stan said resting a comforting hand on my shoulder "He died a noble death saving Marc and fighting for the right cause"

It sounded like he was comforting himself more than me, but I felt better and tried to think of something else while he went back to the bags.

Eventually I pulled myself to my feet as Marc came back, looking a little cooler though still somewhat mad.

He pulled on his pack again "We'd best get going"

But his tone was gentler than I'd ever heard it. Stan sighed but started pulling on his pack.

"Ouch!" I jumped slightly as something stung me, I swung my hands at my hip but stopped midair and let out a shocked gasp.

Stan spun around "What?" he asked anxiously.

I yanked the small dart out of my thigh with a shaking hand. Stan dropped his pack and dashed over to catch me before I hit the ground. Dizzily I saw Marc yank his rifle up only to drop it from shaking hands and fall to his knees then side, unconscious.

The next moment I slipped from Stan's limp arms and numbly thudded to the ground as I saw him collapse beside me with a dart in his neck. Slowly my eyes clouded over as I heard strange voices drawing closer.

Chapter 6

Captured

I opened my eyes and sat up. My hands were free, and I felt numbly cold all over. Looking around I found I was sitting on a soft mattress on the floor of a tent. In the centre I saw both Stan and Marc still fast asleep with their wrists locked to a metal support pole.

Strange voices drew closer, and I gulped as I found my legs were still numb preventing me from moving them yet.

Two people stepped through the tent door flap. They were wearing camouflage uniforms without any symbols and didn't look either Reacher or Elite. The man stepped over and shoved the unconscious Marc, when he didn't budge, he walked out again while the woman came towards me.

I frowned. "Who are you?"

She laughed "I am Adreea of the Degwa tribe" and adding a mysterious air "You might know us as Ace'tam"

"You are natives of Ithral?" I gasped.

This was not a situation I had ever imagined being in. I knew Ithral had 'natives' so to say, they were rather advanced, not as far as star-craft yet but still have a fair amount of technology. I also knew that Ithral was mostly uninhabited because the Ace'tam were now very small tribes, scattered around the planet after their dreadful wars in the past. We had not thought any tribes lived in these regions but evidently, we had been mistaken.

Adreea smiled "Don't worry, I know you are Elite, what's your name?"

I was almost lost for words "I am Winta, how do you know I'm Elite?"

She chuckled and jerked a nod towards the unconscious men "You might be wearing a Reacher uniform, but Reacher's don't put Reacher's in cuffs, besides you do look distinguishably different"

"Oh" I looked down at my wrists which were bruised and sore "True, I hadn't thought of that"

She handed me a cup of water which I drank without hesitation. The sedatives sure left one thirsty.

"Why am I awake and not them?" I asked as I handed the cup back.

"Well, you were only hit with a half dart while they got hit with a full one"

I frowned "Why? Aren't the Elites enemies too?"

She laughed "Well, they were armed and dangerous while you were pretty helpless and in cuffs" then she scowled "Plus Elites didn't set off the electromagnetic pulse to shut down their enemies' vehicles killing most of their own people in the process"

I was stunned "Reacher's didn't set the CEMP off, neither did the Elites, we don't know who did"

Adreea scoffed at my comment while she inspected the contents of Stan's medical case "They're Reacher's, believe me it's just the thing they'd do"

Looking around I saw that the rest of our packs were here too, minus the weapons. I struggled to pull myself up onto my stiff knees.

"You don't understand" I blurted out, to Adreea's great surprise and my own. Was I now defending my enemies? It seemed so wrong, but I did care, Stan at least was good, and I knew it wasn't the Reacher's fault.

"It's not the Reacher's! Even they wouldn't go this far!"

She frowned "Like you know anything, you were their hostage!"

With an effort I kept myself up on my knees "I know them enough to know they wouldn't"

Something in her seemed to snap as she spun around bringing a knife to my throat.

"Now you're starting to sound like a Reacher, maybe I was wrong in identifying you as Elite!" her face was inches away from mine and she seemed seething with anger.

I shook my head and struggled to pull myself up onto unsteady legs away from her "I am not a Reacher but I-"

"You'd better stop vouching for them then!" she said savagely shoving me out of her way.

I lost my balance and fell heavily against a support poll. I yelled as my left side hit the metal. Adreea started in surprise, confused as to why her simple actions had caused such a pained response.

I leant against the pole and held my side, breathing heavily as I slipped down to my knees again. Adreea was scowling but behind it I could see some concern, faint thought it was. I felt the wet warmth of blood run down my side. *'Crap'* I thought *'The wound must have reopened'*. With a shaky hand I unzipped and pulled off the Reacher jacket so that it wouldn't get any bloodier. I then remembered that I wasn't wearing a shirt, it had been torn, and Stan must have removed it. At least I still had a combat bra on.

But there was no time for awkwardness or embarrassment as Adreea gasped in shock. Looking down I saw the lower part of my side wound had broken some stitches and was bleeding steadily. The next moment Adreea was kneeling beside me with Stan's medical kit and holding a gauze to the wound.

"Did they do this to you?" she asked, swabbing the ugly area that had mostly stopped bleeding.

I shook my head "I got it...when my fighter crashed"

I tried not to gasp as she applied another gauze and prepared a bandage "I meant the stitches"

"Oh" I said, glancing towards the unconscious Stan "The doctor did those"

"Which one is the doctor?"

"The short one" I replied "He saved my life when the others wanted to kill me"

"Others?" she frowned as she finished the bandage around my torso and tucked it in securely.

"There was a third, the cats got him"

She nodded almost sympathetically and started packing up the kit "We didn't suppose anyone could have survived the crash as well as the storm and cats, you are lucky"

"Lucky?" I almost scoffed but recalled myself, I was lucky. "How long have we been out for?" I added realizing our urgency.

She looked suspicious "An hour"

I was just about to start explaining the mission we were on when she cut in.

"When your friends have woken up you three will be escorted to the captain for questioning"

Without giving me a chance to say anything in reply she stood up and walked out. Behind her the loose door went rigid and an electric pulse ran through the tent walls. They weren't plain canvas obviously and I didn't fancy touching them. But how did they still have power? I knew they couldn't be responsible for the EMP after what Adreea had said accusing the Reacher's of it. Yet somehow their technology had not been harmed. This made me uneasy, but I didn't know what to make of it without being able to inspect the technology myself.

Gingerly I slid over to Stan to see if I could wake him. He groaned and shifted but still didn't wake up. I looked around and saw that Adreea had left a key on Stan's bag. Taking it up I unlocked Stan's handcuffs and hesitated for a moment before doing the same with Marc's. Both slipped to the ground but remained unconscious. I sighed; this might take a while.

It must have been another ten minutes before Stan finally rolled over and opened his eyes. With a start he sat bolt upright then grabbed his head with a groan as he swayed. I held his shoulder to stop him from falling over and he caught my arm to steady himself more. Looking down at me his eyes widened in surprise and confusion.

"Are you more hurt?"

I shook my head to ease his worry "No I'm fine now, a few stitches broke but it's okay"

He looked away "Did you do that bandage yourself?"

I glanced down and it was then that I realized I'd forgotten to put my jacket back on. Oddly enough I didn't feel embarrassed, perhaps it was because I felt comfortable around him. Plus, it wasn't as if he hadn't already seen me like this before, right? I walked stiffly back to the mattress and pulled on the jacket.

"No, one of the natives did"

His head snapped back around "Natives? Where are we?"

"Degwa tribe of the Ace'tam" I shrugged "They drugged us and I'm assuming we are at their camp"

Stan dropped his face into his hands and groaned "No kidding, I feel like my head is going to explode. What kind of dosage on the sedative did they use? I'm not that big a guy"

I chuckled but stopped short as Marc sat up. He looked extremely disoriented then suddenly, gripping the situation, he leapt to his feet.

"What the hell!" he yelled and the next second he was launching at the tent wall.

"No! Don't touch the walls" I called too late as his fist collided with the electrically charged compound canvas. There was a sharp *Zap* he took the shock and flew backwards to the ground.

"You idiot" Stan mumbled with a slight hint of amusement "Can you ever think before acting?"

Marc had pulled himself back onto his knees, breathing heavily and was glaring at Stan.

"You got us into this mess you stupid doctor! If we'd kept going like I wanted to they'd never have caught us but instead you wanted to give the Elite a breather, if she couldn't keep up then we should have left her to the cats!"

I shuddered and Stan looked annoyed. "You know she has a name! It's Winta!"

"I don't freaking care what her name is," Marc said, punching the post.

"Besides" Stan continued defiantly "If we had continued on ten out of ten Winta would have collapsed. And if you had left her behind, we might as well have given up on the mission because she's the only one of us who has a hope of shutting the CEMP down!!"

It was obvious to see Marc didn't appreciate this logic when he didn't reply. I knew in truth he did want to shut the CEMP down as he cared about the possible other Reacher survivors in need.

He tried to turn on his wrist band "Their tents electrify but my wristband still won't turn on?"

Stan shrugged "Well your band is fried" and sat down leaning against the central support post.

"But don't you see" Marc said annoyed "They're the ones who set this EMP off, that's why their tech still works"

"I don't think so" I said hesitantly "They sounded as though they believed the Reacher's were responsible"

Marc looked angry and Stan said, "So now what?"

I swallowed "They were waiting for you two to wake up before they took us all to their captain for questioning"

Marc lost it and spun around, I fell backwards in fright barely missing the wall, Stan scooted in between us as Marc exploded in a fresh rage.

"THEY'RE WORKING WITH YOU? I knew I should have shot you when I had the chances!"

Stan held up his hands "Marc just shut up for once, she was hit with a lower dosage than us so naturally she'd wake up sooner..."

He was interrupted as footsteps and voices suddenly sounded outside the tent. Slowly I sat up again, still a bit shaken after being trapped in such a small space with a furious Marc.

The door buzzed as it powered down and fell open to let three camouflage soldiers' step in holding strange looking guns with what looked like crystals instead of magazines.

Chapter 7

Interrogation

"Up you three" The first soldier said harshly "let's get moving and don't try anything, these really sting"

Stan helped me to my feet and all three of us stepped out of the tent into the sunlight to look around at the Ace'tam camp. There was compound tents spread throughout the trees on either side as we walked along a path with two soldiers behind and one leading.

After several minutes of walking, we arrived at a large clearing with a semicircle of five chairs in the middle. We were nudged to the front and found there was an elderly man sitting in each chair. I didn't like how the two elders looked at us, with hatred in their eyes, but the other three looked more sympathetic. The middle one, whom I assumed was the captain that Adreea had spoken of, stood up and walked around us. I desperately hoped Marc would keep his temper under control and that these people would-n't regret not having restrained us.

"So, I'm told we have two Reacher's and an Elite, the only survivors we've come across so far"

Stan took the opportunity to act as spokesperson "Yes sir"

The captain came back to his seat and casually looked us up and down, his eyes rested on my forehead that bore the un bandaged suture.

"Looks like you've been through hell and high water"

I made no reply, unsure if I was supposed to talk or not.

"Allow me to introduce myself, I am Brega Tadrai, Captain of the Degwa tribe, who are you?"

There was silence and I was afraid Marc and Stan were going to be stubborn in this area. Couldn't they tell this was-n't the time or place for standard protocol? If we wanted any hope of being able to shut down the CEMP or negotiate for them to turn it off, then we needed to cooperate.

Lifting my head a little I finally broke the strained silence "Winta Yovacar, Elite Tech Engineer and Strike Pilot"

Brega smiled, "Pleasure to meet you, Miss Yovacar. Now, my daughter informs me there is a doctor amongst you?" he turned his gaze to Stan.

"Stan Whitlock, Reacher Tactical Doctor, Sir"

Brega's eyes turned to Marc who scowled and responded with a simple "Marc!"

Suddenly, I felt the compelling urgency of our task "If I may speak?" I blurted out.

The captain looked at me curiously while most of the other elders looked angered. I was acutely aware of Marc's eyes boring into my head, but I tried to ignore it.

"We are on our way to attempt to shut down the electromagnetic field that is hindering rescue ships from trying to come"

I heard an amused chuckle and, looking over, saw it was Adreea standing by with the guards, a mocking look on her face.

"Likely story, tell me Elite, did they threaten you with death to lie for them?"

I felt my heart sink as Marc swore, and Stan sighed; we weren't going to get anywhere if these people believed that the Reacher's were behind the EMP.

Then suddenly and without truly processing what I was doing I looked back at Brega and asked "Or if you would be so kind as to shut down the EMP emitters yourselves that would be greatly appreciated"

He looked startled and three of the other elders leaped to their feet exclaiming in anger.

"Our EMP? Are you accusing us of doing this?"

"How dare you! An invader!"

"With two Reacher's standing next to you? And you choose to accuse us?"

I kept myself as composed as possible and shrugged "Your compound tents still electrify while these Reacher's wrist bands don't work, how do you explain it otherwise?"

Adreea looked furious "We are powered by crystals, the EMP is clearly a more advanced and sophisticated technology, such as your *friend's* wristbands!!"

I forced a sarcastic smile and saw Stan looking impressed. I decided I'd better continue down the path I'd started on.

"Likely story" I grinned "Seeing as you know so much about its composition, I'm guessing the EMP was set off from a Degwa facility, am I wrong?"

This was the last straw and most of the people around us burst out in angry talk. One of the angriest Elders pulled out a hand stunner and fired it at me. Stan shoved me to the side and took the blast in the process. It landed him on the ground writhing from the stinging shock. Marc lost it when Stan got shot and started swinging punches, levelling people left, right and centre before he too was stunned.

I dropped to my knees beside Stan and held his hand as he groaned in pain. I felt horrible for causing him to suffer by making the Degwa's so angry. I hadn't meant to make them so furious. I had simply wanted to persuade them to aid us in shutting the CEMP down by accusing them of being responsible. I had never believed they were and now was certain they weren't by their reactions.

Captain Brega roared, almost lion-like, "ENOUGH!!!" and an eerie silence fell.

Everyone stepped away from us and the Elders sat down again. The atmosphere was almost unbearably hostile, and the guards handled their stunners with eagerness.

"It is clear to all of us Degwa that we are not behind this EMP attack!" his stern voice was momentarily drowned out by a chorus of "Here! Here!".

He turned to us and stared down at me "Do you know where the facility is?"

"We aren't sure, but we believe so" I quickly assured him.

"And how come you know where it is?" he asked, suspicion thick in his tone.

I saw which mountain range the pulse came from" I hurriedly added "Before my fighter was un-powered and crashed"

There was silence as the captain looked around at everyone as if in silent communication, finally he waved towards us.

"Take the Reacher's back to the holding tent"

Marc jumped up and Stan pulled himself to his knees but a second later six stunners and two dark guns were aimed at them.

The captain smiled "It would be easier if we didn't have to drag you"

Reluctantly Stan and Marc were led off and I felt mildly terrified being left alone with these now seemingly murderous natives.

"Now then, Miss Yovacar, was it? Let's get started" the captain said, sitting down comfortably.

The next hour was spent in what felt like a harsh interrogation. I sat on the ground and had to explain what the Elite's goal was in this attack on the Reacher's and then everything I knew about the Reacher's and this EMP. It only seemed to be Captain Brega who had any inclination to believe me at the start but slowly over time most of the other Elders seemed more inclined to trust my word.

"I understand you were these Reacher's hostage, why then do you defend them?"

I hesitated, I didn't trust Marc, but I didn't want to lie as I did trust Stan.

"Stan is a doctor and saved my life, I trust him"

Brega smiled "And the other one? Marc?"

I hesitated, this did not look good, but I had to be honest with them, it was our only chance.

"You can't trust him!" it was Adreea "That's easy to see because he's the one that had you in the cuffs, was he not?"

I swallowed, I really did not want to defend Marc, I hated him. "He doesn't trust me" I manoeuvred cautiously "To him I am an Elite and potentially dangerous, but he needs me to help shut the facility down as I'm an engineer"

Adreea scoffed in disbelief.

"Please Adreea" Brega said in a tired voice "Watch your tone, you're making me look like a bad father"

Adreea scowled "You are not seriously about to let them go on this made-up errand that is so clearly fabricated? If there was such a generator facility that did not belong to the Reacher's we would have knowledge of it as this is our region!"

"Not necessarily" Brega mused "If there was an explosion at the same time as the EMP went off, like Miss Yovacar tells, then perhaps it is an underground facility"

His daughter did not seem to care about this reasoning and stormed off. I watched her leave in confusion, wondering why she hated the Reacher's so much but not the Elites, we were both invaders to their planet.

"She's understandably angry at the Reacher's" Brega said slowly "They killed her boyfriend"

Now I understood why she had been so friendly to me at the start but, after assuming I was with the Reacher's, she became hostile.

There were a few minutes of hushed talk between the five Elders and guards before he turned back towards me.

"We have decided to escort you off our land blindfolded and let you be on your way to shut down the facility. It is in our best interest that the rescue ships can come and take away their people from our land and planet. We will restore your weapons and supply you with food and water but that is all"

I was almost overwhelmed with relief, "Thank you so much," I whispered before being escorted back to the holding tent.

The soldiers opened the door, and I slipped inside, both men looked at me curiously.

"They're letting us go," I said quickly in excitement.

Marc looked suspicious but Stan enveloped me in a hug.

"Thank you, Winta," he sighed.

I was taken completely by surprise and pushed him off me. He looked apologetic but I quickly turned away embarrassed and grabbed Hank's pack. Stepping out of the tent as we strapped the packs on, we found there were the original three soldiers waiting for us. They held up strips of cloth.

"We need to be blindfolded as they lead us out of their camp," I said faintly having forgotten this detail.

Stan stepped forward willingly, but Marc looked like he was going to lose it again. He must have remembered the sting of their stunners because, to my utter relief, he eventually relented and blindfolded himself.

"He must still have some sense left" I thought as they covered my eyes and spun me around to make me lose my sense of direction.

Twenty minutes of stumbling and guiding later we finally stopped. As our blindfolds were removed, I saw we were deep in the forest. The soldiers placed our weapons down a few meters away.

"Southwest is that way" the leader said pointing in the direction they'd aimed the rifles.

Then they vanished in all directions among the trees. Marc stalked over and grabbed his rifle, two handguns, magazines and several grenades.

Stan shouldered his rifle then turned curiously "What did they want you for?"

I sighed "They wanted to know everything, and they hate Reacher's more than Elites, as you saw"

He nodded understandingly.

I shifted uneasily "Sorry about the stunner, I didn't mean to push them that far"

He smiled "Don't worry about it, I think you did the perfect thing to get them to understand, besides, my fingers stopped tingling a while ago"

He started walking southwest and as I followed, I caught a glimpse of Marc's dark face, he was not at all happy. I was now free and part of their 'team' instead of being a bound hostage, and it was clear this didn't sit well with him. The numbers and dynamic of our group had drastically changed over the course of a few hours and neither of us was adjusting to it well.

Now there were only three of us, I was no longer a hostage, and we were supposed to be all a team, working together and on the same level of respect. I gulped but kept on walking, giving Marc a wide berth.

I was not looking forward to the next few days.

Chapter 8

Free

Despite my drug induced sleep and the hour or so of minimal movement I still found I was extremely weak and exhausted after the morning's excitement and activity. But I forced myself to go on a fast walk without rest for several more hours. As the sun was sinking low Stan called a halt in a good-looking ravine.

Dropping my pack, I slipped down against the rocky wall in complete exhaustion. I just wanted to close my eyes and fall asleep, but I was also starving. Marc sat over the other side and started a small thermal lamp, he had not said a word since we had been freed, and I knew he hated the fact that I was free. He couldn't cuff me unless he restrained Stan, for the tables had turned and I had been freed by the natives. It was a rather awkward situation.

The Degwa packed food and water for us?" Stan questioned as he pulled out a few odd-looking packages and water skins from his bag.

"Oh yeah I forgot to mention they said they'd do that" I replied, too tired to think much of it.

Marc scoffed "What else did you forget to mention?"

My head shot up in anger "You wouldn't want to know half of it!"

He scowled and I would have continued talking about the Degwas dislike for the Reacher's, but Stan intervened by giving Marc an emergency food pack and myself some of the Degwas food.

He then sat down next to me. "What do you think it is?"

I inspected what looked like strips of preserved meat. "Maybe cat meat? I don't know"

It turned out to be very tough but extremely delicious. Along with the meat was some sort of bar or bread, I couldn't tell what, but it was tasteless, and I didn't mind. After eating I settled down to try and sleep in the growing darkness but found that, exhausted though I was, sleep avoided me.

Finally, after tossing and turning uncomfortably for half an hour I sat up and sighed.

Stan was on the first watch and looked over to me.

"Pain?"

I shook my head; the pain I felt was minimal compared to the slight sick feeling that seemed to stick around. I had noticed it before leaving the Degwa tribe and wondered if it was a side effect of the dart sedatives.

"No not really, just can't sleep, I don't know why though.... I'm so tired"

He stood up from where he sat and came over to me holding the thermal lamp. "May I?"

"Sure," I said, pulling my legs in front of me as he sat down next to me and felt my forehead.

"Hm, no fever so I hope it's not an infection, the cough still bothers you every now and then though so we should watch that"

A cool breeze had started blowing and I shivered slightly pulling the blanket tighter around my neck.

"Cold?"

I nodded and accepted the second blanket he offered. Glancing over at Marc who was asleep on the other side of the ravine I gathered my courage and finally asked the haunting question.

"If we do manage to shut down the CEMP" I hesitated and felt his eyes watching me intently "What will happen to me?"

There was a short silence, he looked towards Marc, and I looked up at him.

"I'll make sure you go free to Elita"

Hearing the honesty in his voice I unconsciously let out a sigh of relief but quickly looked away when his eyes turned back to me.

"He won't let you," I whispered with a hint of fear.

It was now Stan's turn to let out a sad sigh "He will, I know he is cruel and harsh and for that I am truly sorry, but he does have somewhat of a heart, you see he's lost a lot"

I looked back up at him while he continued to talk and noticed his usually calm face had changed with sadness.

"Like you, for all he knows he's lost his entire squadron, all his mates and buddies, Hank was his last squad member, unfortunately he deals with grief through anger"

A tear slipped down my cheek, and I quickly wiped it away as I looked back towards the sleeping Commander. For all I knew we'd both lost all our friends from this fight.

"What about you?" I whispered.

"I haven't lost anyone as family to me as Marc or maybe you have, you are the only survivor I found alive and... was able to save"

I knew he was referring to Hank. "I'm sorry, I shouldn't have brought it up"

"No, don't be sorry, it's okay"

The memory also made me feel a bit sicker, so I tried to think of something else. The thoughtful silence was broken by Stan.

"May I ask you something?"

I nodded "I think so"

He seemed a little uneasy. "Do you trust me?"

I was surprised, not having expected such a question and was lost for words for a moment. "I...yes I do, I do trust you" I stammered out.

"So can you answer me honestly?"

I frowned in confusion and looked up at him "What do you mean?"

"How long have you been feeling sick?"

I started but his eyes caught mine. "I I..." I paused but conceded under his steady gaze "Since the camp"

"Symptoms?"

I swallowed "Fatigue, slight abdominal pain that comes and goes as well as a growing nausea"

He nodded "I'm worried that you might be having some reaction to the sedative, that or worse, the infection is returning. Unfortunately, I don't have any antibiotics left after I first stitched you up"

"You need to stop worrying about me so much," I said too quickly.

He frowned "I'm a doctor and you're my patient who is unwell; I'm supposed to be worried about you. If you are getting pneumonia and that cough gets worse before we get rescued, you could be in real danger again"

I shook my head "You're not supposed to be this worried about me" I broke off unsure how to go on.

He leant back and folded his hands in his lap "How do you mean?"

I glanced away from his curious eyes, feeling uncomfortable with the situation I had put myself in. "I just meant... you worry a lot about someone who isn't a Reacher, and I know you've already said that's because you are a doctor and help anyone who needs it ... but still, I am just another patient, are you like this for every patient?"

He was silent and staring up at the star speckled sky with a thoughtful and faraway look.

"I see what you mean but not every scenario goes by the book, they're all different, same as the patients"

I was confused, mostly at myself, because I wasn't even sure what I was trying to say or get at "But haven't you saved lots of people's lives?"

"Yes," he nodded "Though I've lost many I've saved probably over two hundred" his eyes turned back to me with an intrigued gleam "But I've never saved a Winta Yova-car before"

I felt more uncomfortable, unsure where this was going, so I tried changing the trajectory a little.

"But you have saved other Elites before, Elites that have killed Reacher's just as I have? Marc's treatment I can understand but not yours...I just don't understand"

He seemed to wander off in thought again before answering slowly

"There is no good side or bad side, if anything there's just two bad sides. It's taken my whole life so far to figure it out myself and it has shaped who I am and how I live, it's helped make me who I am now"

His eyes fixed me again but this time I didn't break the contact. I felt so much respect for this Reacher and what he had said seemed so confusing, yet I felt I understood most of it. My mind wondered about his planet Recharva, his people and his family and what they were like. I thought of what he'd said about no good side or bad side and wondered what kind of person I would live to be if I was ever rescued from Ithral.

Suddenly I was pulled from my deep thoughts by a quiet voice asking, "Are you alright?" and I realized I was still staring at him.

He smiled faintly, I blinked and looked away, oddly enough I didn't feel uncomfortable this time.

"I'm fine," I added vaguely, still a bit lost in thought.

He chuckled "Are you sure? Because you didn't seem quite all there"

I frowned. "Well, I don't think I was all there"

"What were you thinking about?" he asked, now curious.

"I was just wondering if you have a family and..." I'd said it out loud without realizing it and hurriedly added "I was just wondering, you don't have to answer, I'm sorry I shou...."

"Winta, it's fine" he interrupted politely and, looking up, I saw he was smiling again.

"My mother and father are retired and live on a holiday island; they were rather successful in their business and now casually council people and attend advisory meetings. My older brother is in the ground force and my younger brother is somewhere on Reacharva doing some form of study, don't ask what it is because I can never remember" he chuckled before continuing "My older sister is also a tactical doctor, I believe she's stationed on the Atravo moons where there is some civil fighting currently happening"

I noticed a little sadness in his eyes, but his features and attitude seemed to brighten up as he spoke of his family.

"I only have one brother," I mentioned. "Though I do live with a roommate, she's kind of like a younger sister I suppose"

"What does she do?" he asked curiously.

"She's an accountant"

"And your brother?"

"Oh, I think he still works in Elitas star craft factory" I answered thoughtfully, trying to remember my life, it felt so long ago, almost the life of another person.

"My parents are working in the fighter pilot training division on Elitas second moon, Detra"

As I finished this the homesickness returned and I tried disguising my emotions in a fit of coughing. Once again, I underestimated Stan's observation skills, he picked up on my change in mood and extended an arm, offering comfort. I hesitated, unsure what to do, I wanted to but... I gave in and leant against his shoulder as he wrapped an arm comfortingly around me.

Homesick?" he asked, strangely soft.

I nodded, still fighting tears. "I...I just want to go home"

"We all do" he said as he rubbed my arm, to my surprise it calmed me down.

I swallowed "I'm sorry I got angry at you when you asked about Elita"

He chuckled "You don't need to be sorry, your reaction was perfectly justified, I shouldn't have let my curiosity be so careless at such a time"

I sighed; I wasn't going to argue with him when he was mostly right.

"I just hope that..." he paused thoughtfully, staring up at the stars "That something good comes from all this, maybe a truce or better yet, full out peace"

I let out another sigh avoiding a cough "I do wish for peace; this war has ruined too many lives already. Do you think it's possible?"

He shrugged "I pray it is"

I'm not sure how long we sat like that for but gradually I started to doze off and finally, fell asleep.

I woke up stiff and sore but worst of all was the heaviness in my lungs and the unpleasant nauseous feeling in my stomach. I found I was lying on Stan's jacket as a pillow. Pulling myself up sitting I rubbed my eyes and coughed, it had been easier to breathe when I had been lying down.

Looking around I saw Stan was repacking the bags and Marc was holstering his weapons. I pulled myself to my feet a little unsteadily and, after rolling up the two blankets, gave them to Stan who strapped them onto Hank's pack.

He smiled as I handed back his jacket. "How'd you sleep?"

"Well, thank you" I answered as I accepted the food and drink, he offered.

I managed the water alright but when I tried to swallow some food I burst out in a fit of coughing and just managed not to vomit as phlegm caught in my throat.

Stan jumped up and caught the cup as I dropped it to clasp my aching side "What's the matter? Still not feeling well?"

When my coughing finally subsided, I managed a feeble nod and painfully swallowed to keep down a few mouthfuls. I guessed Stan was going to suggest some more rest or something, but I shook my head.

"We have to keep going, I'll be fine, it's just a cough"

Though his face showed disapproval and concern he did not protest and instead helped me clip on the backpack after removing a few items to make it lighter.

Marc hadn't said a word, but I saw him cast a few interesting glances at me. I supposed he was wondering when he'd need to *put me down*. With this pleasant train of thought we set off southwest into the woods. The heaviness in my lungs soon started to affect my breathing and I coughed more often but I did my best to not let this slow my pace.

It was a dark cloudy day, and a chilly breeze was blowing as we continued, slowly but surely drawing closer to our goal.

Stopping for a break around midday I discovered I could no longer eat at all. I couldn't stand the taste of the meat as it made me gag nor could I swallow the bread as it was too grainy and made me cough. My nose ran annoyingly, and the phlegm was slowly growing more regular. I could see the clear and almost tortured worry in Stan's eyes but there wasn't anything he could do, and this only made everything worse for him.

Setting off once more, I barely remembered the afternoon as we pushed on. I also don't know how I found the strength to keep going but I did.

When darkness came, we stopped and set up camp under the shelter of a large rock. Stan tried to offer me food, but I knew it wouldn't go down, so I had to refuse. I drank all the water I could knowing this was my best bet at survival.

"You need to eat something," Stan said desperately.

I huddled under the blanket and coughed "I can't eat it Stan, I can't swallow it"

My lungs were feeling the exhaustion, and my breathing was more laboured with a faint wheeze every now and again. This worried Stan and his anxiety was not helped by Marc's restlessness.

"We ought to push on through the night!" he growled.

Stan scowled "The mountains are still at least half a day's journey away and we've no way of keeping track of our trajectory!! You should know this!"

"We would have made it there already if you'd left her with the natives," Marc muttered.

I cringed; it was obvious Marc still hated me for being such a drag on their progress.

"We need her help to shut the facility down!" Stan shot back less calmly.

Marc's silent hostility was really getting on his nerves now and I wondered why. Why was he suddenly so much more defensive when he'd let Marc push me around so much before? I didn't know why but I was too tired to try and figure it out, so I just curled up and tried to sleep. This was extremely unsuccessful, and the night was spent in restless slumbers with much tossing and turning between fits of coughing.

Chapter 9

Facility

I must have slept at some point because I woke up coughing. Sitting up I found Stan trying to give me a drink which I struggled to swallow. Once again food was a lost cause, and I felt nauseous, but this didn't stop me from strapping on the backpack and starting out once more with the others. The mountain range was close now and we were sure to reach the facility by this afternoon. I prayed I'd make it and that we'd be able to shut down this CEMP. Every moment felt like more lives lost.

Most of the time was spent in distant silence with only Marc correcting our trajectory twice. I wondered if he would see me differently if I helped them shut this facility down. Would he see me as a friend instead of an enemy? Not that I thought we'd ever be friends, but anything would be better than a prisoner. Even just a little respect so that he might let me go. I tried not to let my hopes get too high as I still expected him to take me hostage when a rescue ship showed up.

Emerging from a thicket of forest and climbing up to the top of a grassy rise we stopped and gazed out at the scene that met our eyes. Before us stretched several kilometres of loose forested plain that was half burnt down. The terrain slowly started rising into the mountain range and grew more forested as it rose. It was now that we caught sight of the facility. It was mostly hidden under the ground and revealed to our view by a large landslip. It looked like something in the facility had exploded underground as there was now a gaping hole in the side of the foothill. Many trees on top of the hill had fallen over or burnt down and what looked like one external emitter was now visible.

"What happened here?" Stan asked in astonishment.

"I believe something was overloaded when the pulse first went off," I said slowly.

"We have to hurry," Marc said and started down the hill into the burnt woods. Stan gave me a concerned look, but I did my best to ignore it and followed Marc.

Reaching the other side of the burnt forest we stealthily approached the opening of the facility. Its entrance would have been perfectly hidden from sight by the trees and rocks, but all this had been brought down in the landslide leaving it wide open.

"Watch that second door" Marc pointed it out to Stan who redirected his gun cautiously. We left most of our packs hidden behind some rubble and slowly advanced. Finally, we silently stepped through the debris into the dark entrance and let our eyes adjust.

"This landslip can't be more than nine days old," I whispered, looking around and trying to recognise the building materials and architectural style. "This damage must be from when the EMP first went off, either from an overload or some craft crashed into it."

Stan nodded "I'd say the first as we haven't seen any star craft wreckage"

"This isn't Reacher" Marc said looking over a few burnt control panels and the twisted door frame.

"It's not Elite either" I added puzzled, tracing the patterns on the walls of the hall with my hand.

"Then whose is it?" Stan asked.

Finally, I found a control panel that wasn't buckled, markings on it made me do a double take "It's...it's Ace'tam..."

"What the blazers?! But those savages claimed it wasn't theirs!" Marc punched a wall "Should have known they'd lie!"

I shook my head as Stan looked over my shoulder "Look here," I said, pointing at some markings that decorated the control panel. "It's similar to the Degwa tribe but not the same, remember there are many different tribes within the Ace'tam people. This looks older by maybe centuries"

Stan traced a few patterns "You're right, so this is an ancient Ace'tam tribe?"

I nodded. "I'd estimate this facility is about a hundred years old, most likely back when the Ace'tam were having civil wars, but then why did it go off now?" I paused for a couple of coughs before continuing "Either someone manually set it off or..."

"Or?" Marc asked impatiently.

"It was triggered by our star crafts entering radar proximity"

"But our Reacher base had been set up in the North for three weeks" Marc said confused "Why hadn't it gone off before?"

I shrugged "My best guess from what I have heard of these things is that not enough radar signatures would have been picked up to trigger it before, not until both of our star crafts converged to fight"

"Not that it matters," Stan said slowly.

"Can you shut it down?" Marc asked bluntly.

A sudden rumble shook the ground slightly and I caught the panel to steady myself.

"What was that?" Stan asked.

I frowned "An unstable generator tremor? That is not good we need to hurry"

"Can you shut it down?!" Marc repeated impatiently.

I took a deep breath and fiddled with the panel "If we can get to the control room...that is if there is still a control room left, we have a chance"

The control panel wasn't responding but thankfully I saw that the next door was already cracked and open. I hurried towards it, but Stan held me back. Cautiously we followed Marc through it into the next corridor. It was dark but the electric lights on the guns didn't work, and I wondered how we could go on without light when Marc produced military snap glow sticks and we continued. There were a few more tremors and I was not liking the feel of this old abandoned and collapsing facility.

"I can only guess this is powered by thermal converter's and they don't sound stable" I said in worry.

"So, it's going to explode any minute?" Stan asked.

I shrugged "I would have thought it would have done it by now... though I suppose it's slowly getting worse"

"Lovely, walking through a ticking time bomb" Marc grunted.

At the end of the corridor the door was half open and it led into a large airy room with several corridors branching off.

"Our best bet would be going up" I said pointing towards a flight of stairs to the right "No use trying the elevator, it'll either be fried or unsafe with these tremors"

Marc nodded and started up them with me following and Stan bringing up the rear. The stairs felt like they were never going to end, and my leg was really feeling the strain when we finally made it to the top. Sure, enough this was the control room and once again the doors were open. It was dimly lit by a few extremely old globe strips and several lights flickered on the mostly dim panels.

"How come this place still has power?" Marc asked, confused "Why didn't the EMP shut it down?"

"Because the EMP would have ballooned out from the external emitters" I replied as I inspected the room. "So, these facility rooms would never have been touched"

I was grateful the Ace'tam didn't have their own dialect or else I'd only have half a hope with these controls. I groaned and regretted it instantly as it led to a fit of coughing.

"What's the matter?" Stan asked in concern.

"There's good news and bad news" I said when regaining my voice "The good news is that this facility was on a radar trigger, probably set up around a hundred years or something ago and the EMP was set off when it's radar picked up our star craft"

Looking up I could see that neither of them looked greatly relieved, so I continued.

"And I've found out where the generators are"

"And the bad news?" Marc asked, frowning.

I hesitated "I can't shut the CEMP down from here, controls are busted. Someone has to stay here and open the doors while someone else heads down three levels to the core and uses that chip" I pointed to a palm sized control chip in a slot on the bench "To override the safety protocols and manually shut down the generators"

There was a tense silence.

"Why can't we open the doors when we get to them?" Marc asked coldly.

"Because manual controls are on lock-down and I can't turn that off either" I said as I looked over a few dark control panels.

Marc glanced between Stan and me and hesitated for a moment before speaking "I'll stay here with Winta; you take the chip and go shut the core down"

I went stiff, it was the first time I'd heard him use my name and though it sounded odd I was hugely disappointed that he was keeping me here. All my fears redoubled, he was never going to trust me, was he?

Stan was staring at Marc, but I couldn't read his expression. "Winta has to come to the core, I am no engineer and wouldn't have the first idea what to do!"

Marc looked annoyed. "Then she can instruct you from here"

Stan looked exasperated "Our wrist bands don't work remember? How are we going to communicate?"

I felt myself shrinking against the wall. "Not now, please don't fight..."

I saw Marc look at me and wondered if that was a surprised look on his face or if I was imagining it.

"The facilities comms should still work from that control panel with the microphone" I said quickly pointing it out. "I just want to help shut this thing down, can you trust me even a little bit?"

I sighed unsteadily feeling suddenly overwhelmed "Well I don't care if you don't trust me but... I am the engineer and need to go to the core"

Stan seemed undecided about something he wanted to say as though he was trying to come up with other options.

He finally turned to Marc "Why not go with her to the core?" I heard his voice falter slightly; he didn't want Marc going with me "I'll stay here and operate the doors"

I saw something strange flash across Marc's face, something was going on in his head and I wasn't sure if it was good or not. He was eyeing Stan oddly as if he was somehow both surprised and impressed that he had made this suggestion. My best guess was that Marc knew how much Stan mistrusted him around me, and that somehow this trust in him may have changed his mind in trusting me.

"We don't have time for this," I sighed desperately.

At last Marc seemed to relax "Okay, Stan you take the chip and go with Winta, I'll stay here and follow your instructions on which doors to open"

I was so relieved and quickly turned to the comms panel "This panel controls all internal doors," I pointed out the switches. "Each door should have a comms pad; Stan will contact you and tell you the level and code to open the ones we need."

Marc nodded in acknowledgement.

"Thank you" I whispered timidly, he gave me an uncertain look before turning to Stan.

"Good luck," he said, and Stan returned a quick salute before grabbing the chip and followed me out the door.

We descended the stairs and had almost reached the bottom when a sudden tremor made us both grab the rails for support. Reaching the open room again I remembered the directions to the core.

"This door" I pointed to a far left one.

Stan pressed the comm pad button and spoke "Level 4 code 35"

A short moment later a "Copy that" came through the comm followed by the door creaking and finally sliding half open. It was hard keeping track of all the doors and stairs we passed through and descended but I knew we'd gone down at least two full levels. Several tremors had shaken the ground, and they were slowly growing stronger.

As we waited for another door to be opened, I looked around and noted buckled walls and broken supports.

Stan noticed my gaze "Not especially structurally sound hey?"

I shook my head "I'm surprised we've made it this far..." I paused and looked away from him. The gravity of danger we were in had been dawning on me gradually.

"You can say it out loud," he whispered.

A lump rose in my throat and I didn't know what to say.

He took my hand in his and gave it a reassuring squeeze "I've guessed as much by now"

I squeezed his hand back thankful for the comfort it gave "I don't expect any of us will get out of here alive" I looked around uneasily "If it's already this unstable, as soon as we shut down the safety protocols the whole place is going to fall apart at once. There will be nowhere for the power to go..."

The door opened and I began to step through it when he gently pulled me to a stop. "Maybe you don't have to do this"

I stared at him in surprise "What do you mean? We have to shut this down"

He shook his head "I mean maybe *you* don't have to do this"

I frowned in confusion "But *you* don't know how to shut it all down, I need to see the set up so I can figure out the sequence"

"I know," he said with a growing eagerness, "But why don't you give me the instructions, walk me through the process, then you can leave with Marc, and I'll stay behind and..."

I grabbed his other hand tightly "No way, I'm not leaving you here to do this by yourself"

"Winta" he said in a low voice that I'd never heard before "I don't want you to be hurt and if there's a chance to avoid that"

"I know" I nodded "But I don't want to leave you alone" He smiled, and I thought I saw tears in his eyes.

Another tremor brought us back to reality and we both hurried through the door and down the stairs still holding hands. The temperature was noticeably higher and looking over the balcony rails I saw we'd made it to the first floor which was an enormous open chamber.

"Down there" Stan pointed with some awe at the staircases that lead down along the walls to the floor of this huge open room. I could see four generators but only two were working, the third looked as though it was damaged and had been out of order for decades and the fourth had never finished being constructed.

"I'll let Marc know we made it and to get clear" He gave my hand another squeeze before letting it go and went back up the steps to the door.

I clenched my fist to stop my hand from trembling.

The door com clicked "Marc, we've made it to the core"

"Copy that" Came the quick reply.

Another tremor rocked the walls, and I gripped the rails. How long did we have? This could fall apart any minute or it could stay this way for another century, we just didn't know. But what we did know was the rescue ships and survivors didn't have a century.

The com clicked again "Thank you Marc, we are about to commence generator override and shut down, you would be best to get outside"

There was radio silence for a few moments, then a "Copy that" followed by a more sincere "Good luck to both of you, over and out" which ended the communication.

I took a deep breath and turned. Stan reached the balcony and offered his hand. I took it and, with another deep breath, we started the last descent.

The generators were placed in the four corners with rather a large distance between each of them for safety's sake. As we reached the bottom of the last staircase and approached the closest working generator, I noted the debris and fallen structural materials.

"This place has been falling apart for ages now" Stan mentioned. "I wonder why it was abandoned in the first place"

"I suppose we'll never know," I said slowly as I inspected the control panel.

It was several minutes before I let out a relieved sigh. "Okay, if you swipe the command chip through that slit then pull this lever it should shut this generator down" I said pointing out the slot and lever.

Stan took a deep breath and slid the chip through the slot; there was a distant hum. He had to use both hands to pull the heavy lever down. A loud click echoed around the room as the generator slowed and finally fell silent. We both stepped back almost waiting for something to happen then started towards the second generator in a hurried walk. Another tremor shook the ground. This one was the most violent so far as it knocked us both to the ground.

"The converters on the next level down are growing more unstable with nowhere to send their heat" I yelled over the shaking noise.

"Come on we've got to hurry," he called, pulling me to my feet.

A deafening cracking sound made us both look up before diving to the left as a few beans smashed to the ground. Scrambling back to our feet we staggered towards the last generator as the ground continued shaking under us. A stronger tremor was followed by a muffled explosion that made us duck down. Looking back, we saw several generator power cables had exploded and suddenly burst into flames.

"Winta Run!!" Stan yelled and I could barely hear him over the roar of fire and rumbling crash of more falling debris. I spun around and ran as fast as I could but neither of us would ever have been fast enough. Part of the roof smashed to the ground behind us, and I could feel the searing heat of flames burning my shoulder. Something heavy hit me from the side and sent me flying across the floor to stop hard against the wall. My head was fuzzy, and I was partly winded, but I did not think I'd lost consciousness. I struggled to pull myself onto my knees and gasped in pain from the burn on my left shoulder. Frantically I looked around for Stan and couldn't see him. Had he been crushed by the falling rubble? More dust cleared and then I saw him, sitting slumped against the wall a few metres away with some rubble over his legs.

"Stan!" I gasped. Pulling myself over to him I shoved the rubble away and froze in horror. His right leg was broken above the knee and a metal rod was stuck through his left side.

"Winta" his voice was strained in pain "You need to shut the last generator down,"

I slumped in shock at his side, taking his shaking hands in mine. What did the generator matter now? I had to help him before this place completely collapsed.

"Come on Stan, we can still get out of here" I tried to help him up, but he grimaced in pain and pulled me back down to my knees at his side.

"Don't try to move me" he groaned "This rod is fixed to the wall"

"I'll help you off it, we can bandage you up and..."

He interrupted me "The generator!"

"To hell with the generator" I yelled in frustration "This place will collapse on itself, and it won't matter if I've shut it down when that happens!"

"We can't risk it" he said pushing the chip into my trembling hand "It's lasted this long; there's no guarantee it will be destroyed in a collapse"

"But Stan..." I choked on a sob as I realised what he was asking "We can still..."

"I love you Winta" he feebly squeezed by hand "I'm sorry for everything you've had to go through, but you've got to do this"

My eyes filled with tears "But you'll die!" I sobbed "I don't want you to die"

"I'm a doctor, I know when someone isn't going to make it no matter what, at least save yourself"

I shook my head, tears now streaming down my cheeks "But I love you too, I *can't* leave you to die"

"Don't kill yourself for me" he shuddered "Please, I want you to live"

"But I don't want to live without you," I cried.

He feebly reached a blood-stained hand behind my head and gently pulled my face close to his "May I... please?" he whispered faintly.

I could never have imagined my first kiss to be like this, but it felt right, so I let it be. It only lasted a second then his hand dropped away from my hair, and I stared into his teary eyes. He slipped something else into my other hand, I saw it was his Reacher medic badge from his jacket. I hadn't realised they could be detached.

"You have to give this to Marc" he struggled to say breathlessly "And...and tell him I said it was an honour serving under him" he tried to push me away "Now please go... live, live for me"

"Stan please, I don't want to go" I sobbed, dropping the chip and badge and taking his face in my hands.

His eyelids flickered "Winta please"

"Okay I'll go" I choked out heart-brokenly "I'll do it for you"

He smiled and lightly placed his hand over mine. I felt his breathing slow as his eyes closed and his hand dropped away. I lean forward and kissed him through my tears. His breathing stopped and he slumped down against the wall motionless, the faint smile still on his lifeless lips.

"Goodbye Stan" I sobbed, folding his hands in his lap.

The ground shook violently and wrenched me out of my shock. I grabbed up the chip and badge as I pulled myself to my feet, ignoring the sickening pain from my shoulder, leg and heart.

Limping towards the last generator with a hazy vision and mind in turmoil I slipped his badge into a pocket and zippered it tight. Almost collapsing in sobs onto the control panel I fought against the burning pain and tears. Punching in the override sequence I slipped the chip through the slot and used all my strength to pull the lever down, screaming in pain as the effort strained my burnt shoulder.

The shut off click was barely audible over the loud rumbling and shaking of the facility, but the generator slowed and finally died. Struggling to keep my feet I glanced around breathing fast as I realised the fire was burning up the oxygen. Taking one last glance towards Stan's still form I turned and threw myself towards the stairs. The ground was now constantly shaking, and it was a struggle to stay upright as I climbed the buckled stairs. Reaching the doorway, I forced myself onwards and up going back the way we had come, never consciously taking a turn but following a numb autopilot. I could almost feel the facility collapsing underneath me and fought back the choking feeling as I remembered Stan's words.

Finally, I made it back to the first open room and dashed limping through the entrance. Staggering against a few rocks I slid to the ground, exhausted and gasping the fresh air.

"Winta! Where is Stan?"

I looked up and saw Marc rush to my side, strapping his pack on. I opened my mouth but choked on a painful sob.

"He's gone..." I managed, struggling to unzip my pocket and shakily hand him the bloody medic badge. Marc took it and stared.

"Stan said... to tell you... it was an honour serving under you"

I saw the look of anger on his face. The expression of betrayal flashing in his eyes and I knew he blamed me for his friend's death. I wondered if he'd kill me now like he'd always wanted to or whether he'd let me alone to die when the facility imploded. But to my bewilderment and shock he pulled me to my feet, linked my right arm over his neck and started hurrying away from the entrance. I couldn't understand what he was doing, was he saving me? I felt too numb, weak and in pain to be able to think straight so I concentrated as best I could on trying to walk fast.

The ground tremors grew louder and stronger and glancing back I saw the ground and hillside giving way as it continued crumbling into the growing abyss below.

Eventually reaching the relative safety of the grassy hilltop Marc set me down and leant against a tree trunk panting. An ear-splitting screech yearned through the air and looking up we watched the emitter disappear into the gaping hole where the facility had been.

I sighed shakily, "We did it...." I couldn't go on as tears started streaming down my face and I broke down crying realising that this sinkhole was Stan's grave.

The loud hum of star craft engines drew our attention to the sky, and we saw rescue ship after rescue ship descending through the cloud's. My tears turned to that of joy. It wasn't all for nothing, we had done it. I looked back to the smoking sinkhole and imagined what his face would have looked like on seeing this sight and knowing we had succeeded.

"We should get to a clearing so I can send off a flare," Marc said bluntly.

I was lost in thought and didn't register what he'd said.

"Winta, we have to go...he's gone"

I heard him this time and swallowed back my tears but couldn't pull myself away, it was as though I'd lost the will to move. I knew Stan was gone forever but I didn't want to accept it and leaving here would be final.

"Winta?" he knelt by me, and I curled up away from him instinctively. "I'm not going to hurt you"

He said this in a voice that was not his own, gentle and sincere. It didn't sound like it was his and it made me look up in surprise and confusion.

Our eyes met and I finally saw the *somewhat of a heart* behind his that Stan had spoken of.

I knew he was telling the truth; he would not hurt me. A sob caught in my throat and the tears started again as I struggled to my feet. His hand caught my arm and helped me up as I swayed unsteadily, almost overcome with fatigue from my retreat and heartache.

I wasn't sure how long we trekked slowly through the woods for, but it felt like the next moment when we stumbled across a large clearing. A loud shot nearby startled me, and I looked around expecting to have to run for my life until I saw it was Marc's flare gun. He let me slip to the ground and leant against a tree trunk. I wanted nothing more than a hug from Stan, but he was gone forever. At this thought I broke down again and started sobbing uncontrollably.

I almost jumped when I felt Marc's hand rest on my shoulder and went to shake it off when I saw his face. Grave and sad he looked down at me and I realised this was the closest he knew how to comfort someone. He was not good with words and less so with contact, but he was trying and, once the shock wore off, I was able to appreciate his empathy and unified grief. He had lost two comrades, and I had lost someone who had become more than a friend. We were both hurting in this together, so different and yet brought together in pain.

It was not long before the loud rumbling of a rescue ship's engine began descending above us.

Chapter 10

Rescue

The rescue ship was a Reacher vessel. I wasn't surprised because the flare Marc had sent up was Reacher. But as Marc helped me aboard, I was shocked to notice that there were more Elite survivors on board than Reacher's. It was amazing to see peace between both people who had been bent on murdering each other just over a week before.

Marc helped me into a seat and strapped me in as I deftly let him, still distant and trying to grasp everything that was happening. Something cold touched my burnt shoulder and I gasped in pain as I pulled away.

"Easy Winta" Marc held me still "You're hurt, let the medic help"

I gritted my teeth against the stinging cold but held as still as I could while the medic applied a soothing cream then a bandage. Once finished he moved on to the next injured survivor.

Discussions and announcements were sounding all around me, but I couldn't hear anything, my mind was blank as I lean back and closed my weary eyes. I knew I was on a Reacher ship that might very well be heading for a prison on Reacharva right now, but it didn't matter, nothing seemed to matter. I was in that blank state of mind where absolutely nothing meant anything, a hostage or death couldn't phase me. I was completely lost to hope or reason and now oblivious to the pain, physical and emotional. I had faintly grasped the idea that Marc was kind and would set me free but right now I was just floating in despair. It didn't make sense, we'd done it, shut down the CEMP and saved all the survivors, yet I felt nothing anymore. No relief, no joy, no happiness. Just emptiness, sorrow and loss.

I became dimly aware that Marc tried to talk to me twice, but I couldn't hear him or respond. Suddenly I came back to reality and gripped the seat straps as the ship jolted and landed. I wondered how long I'd been phased out for. I knew it must have been hours in hyperspace, but I couldn't recall any exact time frame. If I had slept, it had not been restful.

Marc un-clipped me and helped me out of the ship. I saw, in amazement, that we had landed at Elitas main military base. All around us Elita and Reacher rescue ships were landing and taking off, both working in total harmony together.

"I have to go back to Reacharva," Marc said next to me. I looked up at him, still completely blank.

He looked concerned "You need to go to a hospital" Turning he sighted an Elite medic "You there, this survivor needs attention"

The medic stepped over and took my un-injured arm to help me away.

"Take this" Marc quickly slipped Stan's badge into my hand. "He would want you to have it" He hesitated "Thank you Winta, for everything, goodbye soldier"

I stared at the blood-stained badge in my shaking hand. When I looked back up the nearest Reacher ship that Marc had boarded was now lifting off, he was gone. I felt a strange sort of loneliness, almost as though I missed him too.

"Come Miss, let's get you to the hospital for a check-up"

I shook the medics hand off "I'm fine, I'll go report in, you're needed elsewhere"

He would have argued with me except, at that moment, several medics rushed out of a nearby Elite craft pulling a seriously injured man on a stretcher and called for his help.

I numbly made my way towards the station; there were so many people around that I felt entirely invisible. Everyone was too busy helping the injured or disoriented and I passed unnoticed through the buildings despite my slight limp. Reaching the locker rooms, I found mine and changed into casual clothes pulling a coat over my bandaged shoulder and wincing in pain.

I didn't have the heart to throw out the Reacher uniform despite its blood stains, tears and the burnt hole in its shoulder so I put it in my locker and closed the door. I vaguely knew I ought to go to the hospital. But something in me just wanted to get away from everything, the noise, the people and the stifling hurry and bustle that was now so strikingly unfamiliar. At this time, I only wanted Stan to help and take care of me, but he couldn't, and I didn't want anyone else touching me.

I headed for the public transport station bypassing the headquarters where I should have reported in. Whatever the Reacher medic had put on my shoulder had dulled the pain for a good while, but it seemed to have worn off as I started to feel the throb of the burn.

Boarding a hover train I headed into the city. Strangers looked at me oddly and I wondered why. They couldn't know I was a survivor, could they? I was now in casual clothes. Perhaps it was the scar above my eyebrow, or my messy hair that gave it away. I had not had a shower in over a week and must look filthy. But no matter, I would clean up at my apartment and then sleep. Oh, how I longed to sleep.

The train stopped at the platform, and I exited. Slowly making my way to the apartment building I barely noticed the news reports and announcements over the public screens and speakers. Taking the elevator to the 8th floor, I hesitated in the hallway before stepping through my door.

Seran Fain, my eighteen-year-old roommate, was watching the news as it reported on the miraculous Rescue from Ithral after nine days of inaccessibility and how both Reacher's and Elites were working together in harmony and peace. She looked around and started in surprise upon sighting me.

"You're alive!" she gasped in relief as she jumped up "I've been listening to everything on the news, and I feared the worst! They haven't got a survivor list yet as everyone is still coming in. Oh, I'm so glad you're okay"

She gave me a heartfelt hug, and I tried to hide the pain it gave my shoulder.

"Oh my" she gasped as she stepped back and looked over my face "Did you hurt your head? You look... terrible, are you okay? Should you be here? I thought everyone was meant to go to the military hospitals for emergency care?"

I brushed my fingers across the healing cut on my forehead. My mouth felt dry, and I couldn't seem to find any words. I shook myself trying to recall what I was doing. I looked around and couldn't quite recognise the room. I was in my apartment, but it didn't feel comforting or restful like I had expected, it didn't feel familiar. I felt like a stranger in my own home, and it didn't make sense.

"I'm tired" I breathed quietly at last and was stunned by the sound of my own voice. It was so low and thin, and I was left slightly out of breath by those two words.

She stared at me as I breathed heavily, a worried expression on her face "You look sick"

I tried to slow my breathing but found I couldn't, I was too exhausted, and it was the only way to get enough air.

"Are you sure you should be here?" she repeated, lowering the volume on the screen.

"No" I said shakily staring at the screen which now showed live footage of the sinkhole on Ithral where the facility had once stood "I should be dead"

"Wow Winta, that's dark" Seran said with a nervous laugh "Also a bit too soon in my opinion, don't you think?"

She came over when I didn't respond and took my hand "You're very warm" She felt my forehead "Like burning up with a fever, and your breathing is really horse, I think you're sick"

I shook my head and started towards my room "I just need to sleep, I'm tired..." this sentence ended in a fit of coughing and Seran ran to grab her phone.

"I don't like this Winta, you're not yourself, does anyone know you're back? Is your family coming? I'm going to call them"

I pushed through my bedroom door still coughing and the sound of the news screen died away. For the first time since leaving Ithral it was as if I could actually hear, think and feel everything clearly. My reflection in the large wall mirror caught my attention and made me pause in astonishment. I stared, hardly able to believe that the person I saw staring back was actually me. A thin figure with dark hollow eyes, sunken cheeks, chalky skin, scraggly dirty hair with a neat row of stitches above her eyebrow.

How was this me? How was I still alive? Why was I still alive? What in the universe was I supposed to do now? Everything was so messed up and different, this room didn't feel like my home, this reflection didn't feel like it belonged to me. Tears slipped down my cheeks, and I fought against the emotion as sobs forced themselves free. It felt like my lungs were too small, weak and tired as I gasped for breath between the sobs. My mind raced beyond my control, and I couldn't keep up. Something fell to the floor, and I saw it was Stan's badge that had slipped from my now open hand.

He was dead and gone forever. He could never hug or comfort me again and I wanted him to hold me right now when everything hurt too much. I sank to my knees and held the badge in my trembling hands as I continued gasping for breath between sobs.

My head felt dizzy and the pain in my shoulder had grown worse with every shaking sob. I wanted to lie down but I wasn't sure if it would be easier to breathe if I did. If only I could stop crying and breathe easier, but I couldn't. Everything hurt and Stan was gone.

Suddenly I heard Seran's voice by my side and, looking up through my tears, I saw her frightened face as she held her phone to her ear.

"Winta, I turned away for a minute to call your parents, what happened? Are you hurt? Can I help? What's wrong? You are not okay! I'm sorry Mrs Yovacar" I realised she was now talking to my mum. "Yes, I think she's sick or hurt, Okay, I'll call them right away, I'm so sorry to frighten you, yes, I'll do my best"

She hung up and dialled the emergency number, I saw she was talking again but I could no longer register her words as I felt an overwhelming dizziness wash over me and the next moment I blacked out.

Chapter 11

Hospital

I came too and found myself breathing hard still on my bedroom floor. The pain in my shoulder was excruciating as I lay on my left side, so I rolled onto my back.

Seran was kneeling next to me talking rapidly into the phone "Yes she's an Ithral survivor, no I don't know, she just showed up, I asked but she didn't answer me, it's like she could only hear half of what I was saying, what was that? Oh yes, I can hear them now, I'll open the window for them"

She jumped up and I looked over as she slid the large window open. It was then that I could hear the sirens growing louder. The next moment a hover ambulance pulled up and two medics climbed through. Everything seemed to happen in a rush now. They knelt beside me asking questions I could not answer while feeling my wrist and neck. I was then rolled onto a stretcher which made me shriek in pain as one of them moved my left shoulder. The next instant he'd un-clipped my coat and was inspecting the bandage.

"She's got a dressing over a burn on her left shoulder" He said to the other medic who was busy slipping an oxygen mask over my face and strapping me into the stretcher.

"She's in shock and panicking too," someone said.

I could hear them start questioning Seran as I was lifted and handed through the window into the hover ambulance. I tried to keep up with what was happening but found it a struggle. Someone cut the coat off my arm and removed the bandage. Then something was stabbed into my right arm, and it instantly settled my breathing back to a normal pace. My head started to feel light and fuzzy and all the pain and weakness in my body steadily evaporated. Time felt much quicker than it actually was and I heard everything while feeling nothing.

They hurriedly carried me through a hallway. There were people everywhere. Then I was placed on a bed. Next a doctor was looking at my eyes, forehead, shoulder then listening to my chest.

I clearly heard him say "She's got a lung infection plus she is suffering from extreme undernourishment and exhaustion; I'm surprised she's still alive in this condition"

I thought I blacked out again and when I came to again, I vaguely felt someone was cutting my shirt off. I heard a gasp, but I couldn't open my eyes properly.

"Doctor!" a voice called in shock.

"That the heck!" I heard him exclaim "How? Who could have done this to her side? She was trapped on Ithral for nine days!"

Faintly I felt scissors again.

"Sir she's got another suture down her leg"

There were more exclamations of shock and amazement.

"They look skilfully done, and only a few places are infected, I can't believe it, it's a miracle she's even here"

I fought against the numbness for as long as I could but finally my eyes fully closed, and my consciousness faded off into a fitful sleep riddled with disassociated dreams.

The room was dimly lit when I woke up and opened my eyes. Glancing around I recognised the surroundings and realised I was still in the hospital. The IV in my arm and the beep of medical monitors next to the bed confirmed this.

I sighed as I recalled how I'd gotten here. Poor Seran, I shouldn't have made her go through that. I knew I ought to have gone right to the hospital, but I wasn't in my right mind. It was much easier to think of what I should have done now, when I wasn't numb from pain and shock.

Feeling some movement of the blankets, I looked to my left and saw that a person was sitting on a chair and leaning heavily against the side of my bed. They seemed to have also been sleeping and were just now waking up.

"Eradan?" I whispered in happiness, recognising my brother.

He sat up with a gasp of relief "Winta?"

I winced as he enveloped me in a hug.

"We were so worried about you when the reports of what happened on Ithral came through"

Just then the curtain was pulled aside and Eradan stepped up to let the doctor and a nurse approach the bedside. Seeing me awake the doctor smiled broadly.

"Good to see you conscious, how do you feel?"

I hadn't really thought about it before but now that I did, I found I felt strangely calm, rested, fresh and clean.

"Much better thank you"

He nodded to the nurse who put a tray of food on the bench before leaving.

"Would you mind if I do a quick check-up?"

I shook my head, and he sat on the chair Eradan had vacated.

"Alright then let's see how you are recovering"

He proceeded to feel my pulse and run over the usual inspections.

"Any pain on the shoulder?"

I shook my head.

"Feeling sick at all?"

Again, I shook my head, and he smiled in satisfaction.

"How is she?" Erad asked with a concerned note.

"She is doing much better than when she first came in and recovering miraculously well considering the extent of her injuries"

"Extent of her injuries?" Erad nervously smiled and tried to sound jovial "Why, they can't have been that bad, Winta's a brick after all"

The doctor looked at me questioningly and I nodded my consent. He took a deep breath and looked over his clipboard as he began.

"Well, she has evidence of three fractured ribs, internal bleeding, a collapsed lung, a tear on her left leg, an open wound on her left side as well as the cut on her forehead and burn on her shoulder."

He took a breath and continued and Erad's face had lost the smile.

"In addition to these she is also recovering from a serious lung infection as well as several wound infections on her side and leg. And to top it all off she is extremely nutrient deficient and malnourished"

I glanced at my brother and saw his now pale face watching me with a ghastly expression.

"My God..." he breathed and leant against the wall almost overcome with emotion.

The doctor smiled and stood up "But as I said before, she is out of danger and recovering miraculously well"

The nurse popped her head around the curtain "Excuse me Mr Yovacar? Senior Yovacar is on the line for you"

Erad shook himself and forced a smile, giving my hand a reassuring squeeze he turned "Mum and Dad wanted to be here, but they couldn't get the flight off Detra, all the star ships had been redirected to the military ports"

I nodded understandingly and he left for the phone call. As soon as he was gone the doctor sat down again with a very concerned and serious look on his face, if not somewhat mystified and curious.

"I'm not going to hide my astonishment or shock that you are still alive, when I first saw your injuries and the medical attention they'd received, I knew only a highly trained professional could have saved your life. But I have no idea how such skill could have been acquired during the situation on Ithral"

I sighed as I lean back against the pillows and took a deep breath.

"It was a Reacher tactical doctor." despite my best efforts my voice was not steady, and I wished tears would stop threatening.

The doctor's surprise was noticeable, and I wondered what explanation he had expected.

"A Reacher? A Reacher saved you?"

I frowned and looked up quickly "Why is that so hard to believe? He was a doctor, and doctors save anyone no matter who or what!"

My tone had turned harsh, and I was surprised at my own annoyance. The doctor sensed my change in emotions and quickly apologised.

"I'm sorry if I've upset you, I didn't mean it in a rude way, I was merely surprised"

He stood up to leave and I suddenly remembered a question I had wanted to ask.

"How long have I been here?"

"Three Days" he answered, checking the dates on the clipboard. "We kept you sedated for the first two to aid your recovery as you were in really bad shape"

I closed my eyes and sighed, I wasn't even surprised, somehow it felt that long, oddly enough.

"Oh, I almost forgot" he added, turning back from the curtain "Your roommate sent this little package"

He handed me a small paper wrapped box before stepping out and closing the curtains behind him. I unravelled it and found Stan's medical badge. The note that came with it read *"You dropped this in your room, I don't know what it is, but I thought you might want it back, get well soon. Seran"*

I smiled as tears slipped down my cheeks, and I held the badge in both my hands. At least I still had this. Sometimes I wondered if it would have been better if Marc had never given it to me, it hurt so much. But I knew, at the end of the day, it was better that I had something to remember him by other than the ache in my heart and the scars on my body.

Erad's strong hand rested on my shoulder, and I started in surprise, I hadn't noticed him re-enter.

"What is that?" he asked curiously, sitting down.

"It's a Reacher medical badge," I whispered shakily.

"Who's it from?"

"The doctor who saved my life"

"Ahh" he nodded "I heard he was a Reacher, I would like to meet him some day, what was his name?"

Fresh tears slipped down my cheeks and my fingers curled tightly around the cold metal.

"Stan Whitlock ...but...but he died" here I couldn't hold the sobs back anymore and they broke through.

"Hey easy Winta, I'm sorry, I didn't know..."

He shuffled the chair closer to the bed and pulled me gently against his chest rubbing my back comfortingly.

"It's okay to cry, you don't have to try and stop it"

I sobbed miserably "But why did he have to die? Why?"

"I don't know," Erad said slowly. "We may never know, but perhaps it would be better asking why didn't you die?"

I took a shaky breath and sniffed "I didn't die because he saved me"

"And why did he save you?"

"Because...because I was hurt and he was a doctor and... and doctors save anyone no matter who they are"

Erad rubbed my arm as I continued crying. I remembered when Stan had comforted me like this. It had been very different from my brother, still so comforting and calming but in a different sort of way, a better sort of way.

I missed Stan and knew I always would. It felt completely confusing and ridiculous but also right at the same time. We had only known each other for nine days. It didn't make much sense to me, yet I had grown to love him even if I hadn't realised just how much till that horrible last day. I remembered how he had kissed me, the gentle touch of his hand through my hair, his voice when he'd asked first. Everything he had done, if possible, he had first asked if he could. But right now, with all my broken heart I wished that he had never saved my life.

We must have stayed like this for around ten minutes over which my sobs slowly faded, and I grew calm and quiet. Eventually Erad sighed sadly and pulled away, lowering me back against the pillows. I yawned and slipped further under the blankets as the exhaustion from crying was slowly making me drowsy.

"I'm sorry Winta" he said, giving my hand a squeeze "I have to go back to work now but I will come back and see you tonight. Mum and Dad are coming from Detra tomorrow and will be taking you back to their home"

I tried to smile as I waved goodbye but ended up swallowing a lump trying to rise. I didn't want him to leave, I felt so lonely and tired.

I tried to eat some of the food the nurse had brought but didn't much like the taste. The doctor returned for another check-up and soon after he left again, I drifted off to sleep.

Chapter 12

Recovery

Erad had come back that night as promised and brought with him my favourite meal and dessert, Lasagne and jam ice cream. As we ate, he told me all about what had happened outside of Ithral during those nine dreadful days.

He explained how contact with the squadrons had been lost directly after a massive energy pulse had been detected on sensors. Shortly afterwards, reconnaissance fighters also dropped off the radars and communications. Finally, they were able to assess that some form of EMP had been set off and there was now a steady continuous electromagnetic field up that would fry anything electronic upon entry.

This discovery resulted in chaos between the governments of Elita and Reacharva as each accused the other of doing this atrocity. But through desperate negotiations and diplomacy it was finally agreed upon that neither was to blame. Soon a peace truce was reached and both peoples began working together on the rescue mission. They settled on a plan to send rescuers and supplies in on foot. They also formed and dispatched a specialised strike team with the goal to find and disable whatever was the source of the CEMP via ground.

Four rescue parties consisting of equal numbers of Reacher's and Elites started searching from the north and east. But all efforts were forced on hold as a huge three-day storm hit the region and the rescuers themselves had to bunker down for survival. This was a suspenseful time for the citizens and families of Elita and Recharva as the governments had no news and little hope to convey. Because of course, no contact could be kept as all electronic equipment was shut down the instant the teams stepped into the field.

Then, on the sixth day after the EMP went off the first team returned to the forward operating base with twenty four survivors, several bodies and a partial list of dead and missing. This news was broadcasted far and wide across Elita and Reacharva and received with cheers or joy and relief overshadowed by a nation-wide grief and mourning.

Nothing else was heard or seen from any of the other teams until the ninth day when, suddenly, the CEMP field faulted and shut down. A huge sinkhole was found to have opened up in the southwest region and experts believed the CEMP facility had been stationed there.

From the instant the first confirmation of the CEMP being down came through, it only took a matter of half an hour before all the rescue transports were launched, collecting survivors and evacuating. He also explained that diplomatic contact had been made with the Ace'tam and that peace treaties and agreements were made saying that Elita and Recharva would never return.

We had finished eating a while ago and Erad now sat back, took a deep breath and asked me about my time on Ithral. I did my feeble best to recount the basic events while leaving out almost everything regarding Marc's treatment and Stan's friendship. I nearly came to tears twice but pushed through without breaking down, it was easier when I didn't tell the harder things. He guessed I was leaving out a lot of details and gave me a hug while I struggled to continue talking through the last day. Finally, I finished, and we sat in silence for several minutes.

We were interrupted from thoughtful processing as a nurse asked to enter. She showed three military officials in and then left. I recognised the third as one of my flight officers and was overwhelmingly grateful to know he had survived. They introduced themselves while expressing their relief that I had survived and the gratitude every other survivor owed me for finding and shutting the CEMP down. I was confused wondering how they had known it was me but then recalled that Marc would most likely be responsible for this information.

They then handed me a tablet and asked if I could document a mission report about my experience on Ithral. If I was willing to of course. They also informed me that the tablet held information on my survivor support fund. I hesitantly took it and told them I would do my best. I was very familiar with standard protocol for mission reports but this time I did not want to follow them.

As soon as they had left to visit other survivors Erad gave me another hug and told me I didn't have to if I didn't want to. Or if I wanted to, I could just write what I had told him. He knew there were a lot more details to my story that were too painful to retell. I was grateful for his support and sad to see him go again. I felt a dreadful loneliness in that room, and he helped ease it.

The usual doctor checkup occurred, and I was given discharge papers for the morning before being helped to sleep with medication.

I woke up almost happy, today I would be leaving for Detra with my parents and staying at their place till I recovered. I sighed as I slowly and gingerly stood up off the bed but smiled as the nurse entered to help me do my exercises. As I stretched through my routine I thought back over my conversation with Erad. What in the worlds was I supposed to do now? I had no idea apart from resting and letting my wounds heal. The war was over, and we were at peace with Reacharva. Ithral was removed from the mining list, and I didn't know if our leaders had any other unclaimed planets under their jurisdiction that they would dare aim at so soon. Stan's dream of peace had come true and I myself was grateful but somehow there were no feelings of joy or happiness. It had cost so much.

"You're doing great" the nurse said as I stiffly walked around the room without her help.

Making it back to the bed I sat down and dropped my face into my hands. I felt so weak and exhausted, would I ever fully recover? Would I ever be able to walk again without losing my breath? The curtain opened and the doctor walked in.

"Good morning Winta, your parents are here"

Looking up I saw them both standing in the doorway with concerned yet relieved expressions on their faces. They stood for a moment staring at me. I guess I didn't look much like the daughter they had seen six months ago just before I was dispatched on mining escort missions.

"Oh Winta, we were so worried" mum said as she hurried to my bedside.

The nurse and the doctor left pulling the curtain closed behind them. mum sat next to me and hugged me gently while dad stood on the other side, a calm hand on my shoulder.

"How do you feel?"

I shrugged "Alright I suppose, just so weak and tired"

Dad patted my un-bandaged shoulder "Don't worry, we're taking you to Detra where you can rest and heal"

Mum choked on a sob and held me a little tighter "Oh darling I read the medical report...your injuries were... horrendous"

I chuckled slightly "You don't have to tell me"

She sighed in relieved happiness "I'm so, so grateful you are alive! I can't believe what you had to go through"

I leant against her shoulder and squeezed her hand "Neither can I... neither can I"

Half an hour later I was leaning heavily on my dad's arm as we left the hospital to the cheers of remaining patients, nurses, doctors, and citizens passing by. Taking a train to the spaceport, we waited in the terminal for our ship.

Planet life seemed to have almost gone back to normal, as though we had never been at war. It was strange, but the good kind.

My parents had already gotten everything from my apartment and military locker and sent it off on the cargo ship. It had been a little awkward when I had gotten the phone call asking about the Reacher uniform in my locker. But I had managed to convince them to keep it and send it along with my other things, after being washed and decontaminated.

I looked around at the various ships and remembered the day I had landed with Marc. I wondered what he was doing and how he was recovering. The thought was almost amusing as I could not help but imagine his version would look more like a gym and punching bags.

I felt sorry for him, even after everything he had said and done to me. He had felt so much more human that last day and I had seen the pain and grief in his eyes.

I was pulled out of my thoughts as our ship opened for boarding. Suddenly I heard my name and turned to see Seran had arrived to say goodbye. I thanked her for helping me and she said she hoped to see me again soon, but I couldn't promise anything.

We had high class passes and got a ship room to ourselves, not that the flight was a long one. Detra was its first stop and only a two-hour flight away. But still, I appreciated the privacy bought by my parents' status. Especially as most the passengers guessed I was a survivor and wanted to talk or express their condolences and gratitude. I was grateful it was not publicly known that *I* was personally responsible for the EMP shut down, it felt like that would have been too much to manage. As it was, there were not many survivors, and everyone wanted the honour of talking to one. Thankfully, my dad knew me well and shut any interaction down politely and swiftly while shielding me from the unwanted attention.

Arriving on Detra we got into dad's hover car which already had my belongings, packed by an assistant. It would have been quicker to get a direct drop off, but my parents believed the drive would be better for me. They were right, I did enjoy the scenery and peace of the trip, and it helped to ease and ground me.

Three hours later we arrived at my parents' house. It stood up in the forested hills above an ocean inlet that was riddled with small tree covered islands. The military training outpost that my parents worked in was only a thirty-minute drive away at the nearest town. They had been re-designated as 'Defence Trainers' now.

As we got out of the car, I smiled remembering how much I loved this house. I had grown up here and so many sweet memories were held in and around it. Dad carried everything into the house and Mum took no time at all to unpack and put my things away. She put the Reacher uniform through the wash again, still not trusting that it was free from blood.

After having dinner, I went to my old room that was upstairs with a small balcony looking out over the inlets. The stairs were not too hard to climb but I felt exhausted by the top. As I changed to bedclothes I looked over my scars in the mirror. They were healing well and even the past infected points looked almost cleared up as I changed their dressings. I studied the scar on my forehead. Out of all the wounds it was the best healed and the least visible. Stan had taken so much care to get the stitches done well to prevent as much scarring as possible. Taking his now clean badge out of my pocket, I sighed and placed it on my bedside table. Flicking off the lights I slipped under the blankets and got into a comfortable position.

Though I was exhausted from the trip and adjustments, sleep did not come easy. My mind ran through so many memories I could not seem to have a break. Before long I found myself dwelling on everything I had *not* told Erad. Rolling over I scrunched the pillow in frustration and groaned. Is this what life was going to look like now? Was it always going to be this hard to get to sleep?

I do not want to remember any of it. I wished my mind would forget everything that had happened on Ithral, everything! As I pondered over this desire the memory of how softly Stan would ask *"May I please"* flickered through my mind and I knew I didn't really want to forget him. Then I remembered the apologetic look he would give me every time Marc was mean, and I couldn't take it anymore.

Hopping out of bed I wrapped the blanket around my shoulders and went out onto the balcony. The breeze was cold, but I liked its crisp, refreshing feeling against my cheeks.

I may have been out there for hours enjoying the breeze and sweet scents of the night as I remembered my pleasant childhood. Finally sleep started to take a toll on me and this time, when my head touched the pillow, my eyes closed and actually stayed closed.

The next few days felt like a jumble of time, and I couldn't seem to keep track. Mum stayed home for the first day but as I was capable of taking care of myself, she went back to work with dad, leaving me to myself which, quite frankly, was all I wanted. I walked the beaches and did my best to write out everything I had told Erad on the tablet. It was hard and many times I couldn't continue because of the tears. Sometimes I felt like I could write out the whole thing, word for word, accurately, and be okay. But half an hour later I had to stop before I had another emotional breakdown. Finally, it was done, I knew it was my mission report, but I wished I hadn't had to write it.

One afternoon, a couple of days later, I was up in my room looking over a few old photo albums of my time in the flight academy. I missed my squadron and sorrowfully remembered that only myself and that flight officer, who had handed me the table, had survived from it.

While dwelling on a photo of me and three squadron colleagues I remembered the memorial service that I had watched on live TV two days ago and the honour speeches given of them. The same day I had received a letter of condolence from Elitas President accompanied by my medal of honour. I was pulled from these thoughts as I heard my Mum calling.

"Honey dear there's a live memorial broadcasting on the news"

I sighed "No thanks Mum" she meant well but those memorials only upset me and triggered memories I'd rather keep forgotten.

"But this one is directly from Reacharva"

I froze, a Reacharva memorial service broadcasted live on Detra? This was unheard of! The next moment I was hurrying stiffly down the stairs to the living room. Dad was still at work and Mum was watching the news while making dinner.

"See? It's from Reacharva"

I stood in the middle of the lounge room and stared at the screen as a Reacher official opened the service. I could hardly believe this was happening. The Elita memorial service had been aired two days ago, and I had barely been able to watch half of it before having to leave.

As all the names of the fallen Reacher's were read out, I felt the twist in my throat and tears on my cheeks as they came to the letter W and finally read out "Stan Whitlock, Tactical Doctor". I wondered if his parents and siblings were somewhere in the crowd and I almost choked on a sob. After finishing reading out the names of the fallen, they then announced that fallen and survivors would be receiving medals of honour. For another hour they bestowed medals to all present survivors and the families or representatives of those not present. Many honorary speeches and stories were read or spoken from survivors and officials.

I couldn't keep myself up and had sunk to my knees as the tears streamed down my face when the Whitlock family came forwards and accepted the medal of honour for Stan. His parents and two brothers were there but I noticed his sister wasn't, I guessed she must still be working where the civil fighting was happening.

The service seemed to be to a close when another announcement came out.

"We have here one survivor who personally helped in shutting down the EMP field, Commander Marc Huxley"

I gasped as I saw Marc stand up on the platform. I then recalled that he hadn't been with the other survivors receiving medals of honour, I wondered why. He looked exhausted but determined and I listened in astonishment.

"As you all know I helped shut down the EMP field, but I was not the one to actually shut it down, that was accomplished by Stan Whitlock and an Elite soldier, Stan tragically did not survive and the Elite soldier was left seriously injured"

I couldn't believe that he was saying this...it didn't sound like Marc at all, and he'd kept my name confidential? I was so relieved for some reason I couldn't explain but I just knew I hadn't wanted everyone to know it had been me.

I was pulled from my thoughts as Marc continued.

"I would like to give my deepest regrets and condolences to the Whitlock family, your son and brother was an honourable and brave man, a far better man than I, he risked his own life again and again to help anyone he could, regardless of who they were. The Elite soldier who is actually responsible for finding where the generator facility was and who Mr Whitlock assisted with shutting it down, was saved by his skill and efforts. They are the bravest Elite I have ever met. Throughout the nine days I was trapped on Ithral I learnt the value of true friendship. To the Elite soldier, if you are watching this please accept my apologies for how I misjudged you and my heartfelt thanks for what you have done for me and my people. There are no words to express my gratitude, and I pray you make a full recovery and in time, are able to forgive me."

He then proceeded to commend the rest of his fallen squadron. I couldn't hear anymore, my mind was running too fast to keep up. Weakly I got to my feet and stumbled up the stairs till I reached my bed, collapsing on it I curled up into a ball and broke down completely.

Sleep had been a struggle since I left the hospital and tonight was no exception. Mum brought me dinner, but I couldn't eat. She was worried for me as she knew I was suffering from PTSD, but so far, I had refused to attend my therapy sessions.

"Honey, we have to take you to the doctors at the end of the week for a checkup and I'm not going to let this go on any longer, I want to help, you need to attend therapy"

I buried my face in the pillow to smother the sobs. I wasn't going to argue with her, not when I was already having a breakdown and knew she was right. Tonight, I wished more than ever that Stan was alive. I just felt that if he was, I wouldn't be suffering as I did. His death nagged at my mentality more than anything else, there was always the doubt of what else could I have done? Could I have done more? Could I have saved him? I was too distraught to think if these questions were reasonable or not. I just wished he was still alive; I missed him more than I could ever explain and I couldn't even understand all the reasons why.

Why? Why? Why? Why? I hated the word, yet I couldn't stop asking it.

Chapter 13

Peace

2 months later

I sat on a log digging my toes into the cool sand and enjoyed the soft breeze as it whipped my loose hair about my face. Looking up I smiled at the glistening waves that gently rippled against the inlet shore with gentle splashes. The soft light of the sunset shone through the trees and turned the water into sparkling pinks and oranges. This was calming and my heart resonated in peace. Life was beautiful. I sighed in happy contentment and watched a few seabirds fly far overhead. It felt like such a long time since I had regretted living.

The past two months had been a whirlwind fight against my PTSD, anxiety and stress but I had come out victorious.

At first, I couldn't make it through half an hour of a therapy session. Again and again, I had resolved to never go anymore but, gently and kindly, my mother and father would coax me to give it another try. Slowly it got better, and I was able to process through my depression and anxieties along with the triggers to my emotional breakdowns.

To help with my sleep I was prescribed medication and an antidepressant. At first, I was too afraid to take them but, after an anxiety attack that lasted an entire night, my mother convinced me to try them. They worked and I was able to sleep more peacefully.

After one week of complete and uninterrupted rest at night I was much more stable physically, mentally and emotionally and began easing off the medications. It was about this time that I also had my last stitches removed. This was done at the training campus by several students and overseen by a skilled female doctor. They were all speechless on seeing the scars. I guessed the experienced doctor had seen worse but maybe not on an alive patient and I was surprised that I found there was something amusing in this.

The removal of those stitches was also like another goodbye to Stan, and I knew he would have been so happy to see how I was doing. I had a lot more peace now and my depression regarding his passing was almost gone. Emotional breakdowns and anxiety attacks were much harder to trigger and lasted for far less time when they did. It was true that I still missed him, and I knew I would forever. But I was grateful to realise that grief and pain no longer had such a strong hold and that their hold would gradually lessen with more time and growth.

I often still had some trouble falling asleep, when certain memories persisted, especially as I adjusted to my lowered medication doses. But slowly, I had come to terms with his sacrifice and the deaths of my squadron members. It was often that I would recall Stan's hope that something good may come from the tragedy on Ithral, and how his hope was granted, and peace had come. His death had not been in vain.

It had taken a while, but I had found there was something still left in my life. Restlessness had slowly stirred up inside me and I found I had to do something with myself. One afternoon, when mum and dad came home from work, they discovered me fast asleep on the couch after I had cleaned the entire house. After this, mum got me a three-day cleaning job at the defence training camp, and I was so grateful. I still had to take it easy as my strength was slow to return and I got exhausted and weak very quickly. But I had something to do and that was a start. The other four days in the week I spent reading, cooking, painting, and walking around the beaches and forests. After a couple more weeks I quit using the antidepressant and sleeping medications altogether, but I did keep a supply, just in case, for some really bad days that came around every now and again.

Coming back to the present moment I hopped off the log and walked through the cool ocean spray heading in the direction of home. I loved these dusk time walks along the beaches. This was my happy place, and I found so much peace and restoration down here.

I took my time climbing the stone pathway back up to the house, enjoying every moment of the closing evening and wondered what my future would hold. I wasn't sure what I was going to do once I was fully recovered. I chuckled a little as I thought of the idea of being *fully recovered*. I couldn't even imagine what that would look like, it seemed so absurd and such a fictional idea.

I was no longer part of the military and had been granted a lifelong survival support fund along with all the other survivors. This meant I didn't actually have to work ever again in my life, but I wanted to and needed to for my own sake.

Reaching the top of the last flight of stairs I looked out at the dimming horizon one last time before going inside. Taking my coat off I hung it on the hook before rinsing off and drying my sandy bare feet.

"Mum, I'm back home" I called as I came into the living room, I stopped in surprise as I saw my brother stand up from the couch.

"Evening Winta how are you tonight?" he asked, smiling.

I had been expecting him in two weeks' time for his birthday, and it took me a good ten seconds to realise that my brother was really here, in person, right now.

"Erad!" I almost screeched in excitement and threw myself at him wrapping my arms around his neck.

"Wow easy sis you nearly knocked me over" he laughed, hugging me back.

"I thought you were coming in two weeks?" I asked half breathless as he set me back down on the ground, I saw his gleeful grin.

"Well, that's what you heard but I was always coming tonight"

"You fiend!" I laughed "You said that all just so you could surprise me by coming early?"

He nodded "You love surprises"

I laughed again as we headed into the kitchen and were greeted by our parents' hugs and joyful grins of happiness.

The next few days were such a joyful time as we all travelled around Detra together and visited our favourite childhood places. We walked through forests, went swimming at waterfalls and quietly wandered along the beaches at dusk. My mind was so relieved by this precious time that I liked to think I was almost fully recovered.

After a full week of exploring and travelling we finally came back home. That was a wonderful night; we had lasagna and my favourite coconut cake as Erad told us all about his new work on the space transports and how everything had been changing since the end of the war. After the wash up, Erad and I went out onto the lounge balcony to enjoy the stars.

"Mother told me all about your recovery, I'm glad you're doing so much better"

I smiled as he slipped an arm around my shoulder "I am glad too, I know I'll never be the same again, but I hope I can be somewhat of the Winta you remembered"

He chuckled "Whatever or whoever you are or turn out to be still won't change how I see you, you will always be my little sister Winta, and nothing can change how I'll love and care for you"

I tried to smile but this time I couldn't, something inside me felt heavy and I wasn't sure what it was at first.

"Erad..."

"Yeah?"

I hesitated "I didn't tell you everything that happened on Ithral"

He nodded "I know, but you never had to and never will have to" with a reassuring squeeze he continued "Somethings don't need to be spoken, especially when their memories are very painful, they are allowed to stay inside you forever"

I swallowed "I know. There are some things I can tell mum but not my therapist or you, and other things I can only tell my therapist and still others that...I only want you to know about"

I didn't want to cry but I started to feel my throat grow tight.

"You can tell me anything you'd like Winta; I'm here for you"

After a few deep breaths I finally mustered the courage to speak my heart "I loved Stan"

I sensed his surprise and felt his concerned eyes watching me.

I wiped away the first few tears "I know it sounds ridiculous... he was a Reacher and...and I only knew him for nine days and..." I didn't get to finish because Erad pulled me into a tight hug.

"Winta its not ridiculous, I am only surprised because I had not thought of it, I thought you were simply traumatised by your time on Ithral, the treatment you received and having witnessed the doctor's death, I never would have guessed it was more, I am sorry"

I sobbed "I am better I promise" I couldn't help but chuckle at how contradictory I sounded "It's just sometimes it's very hard, I miss him a lot but I know now that it's okay, that I can miss him and it's not wrong"

Erad rubbed my back soothingly "Do you want to talk about it?"

I sighed and nodded "You know he saved my life, right?" He nodded and I continued.

"He was really nice, kind and very caring, whenever possible he always asked for permission before he did anything... you know I really liked that, it made me feel so much safer and I was pretty terrified most of the time. He was always trying to protect me from Marc being mean and I felt so comforted when he put his arm around me. I like your hugs, they're safe and comforting and so were Stan's but, I don't know how to explain it, but Stan's were different... better"

I looked up and met Erad's' curious eyes watching my face.

"Do you still hurt inside?" he asked quietly.

I nodded "Sometimes, when I really miss him"

"When are those times?"

I breathed slowly and looked out into the darkness "I don't know, they come and go"

There were a few minutes of comfortable silence until it was broken by Erad's' thoughtful voice.

"Would you like to meet Marc again?"

I started in surprise and my eyes flashed up to his questioningly "Who?"

"Marc Huxley, the Reacher commander from Ithral"

I quickly looked away as I felt my heart begin racing and muscles stiffen, was it because that name still made me a little frightened? I wasn't sure.

"Why do you ask?"

He was thoughtful for a moment, as if thinking on how best to present a proposition "Because he would like to meet you again"

I caught my breath in a gasp. "He *wants* to meet *me* again. Why?"

He shrugged "He says he would like to apologise in person"

My eyes grew wide in confusion "Since when? What do you mean? Wait... how do you know he wants to meet me again?"

"Because he asked me way back when you were in a really bad way so I said no, but you are doing much better now so, if you would like to meet him again, I can let him know that now is an okay time to visit"

I was lost for words. Marc had sought out my brother and asked him if he could meet with me so that he could apologise in person. My mind was so confused, and my memory was all muddled up. It was mixed between his mean Reacher actions and how kind he'd changed on the rescue day. And then again how he had looked, sounded and acted during the memorial service. It really seemed like two or even three completely different people.

"Winta? Are you alright?"

I was pulled from my confused absentmindedness by Erad's gentle shake.

"I'm fine, I think, just a bit confused"

"Okay, because you were quiet for a really long time"

"Really? I didn't realise... Sorry"

"Don't be," he smiled, giving me another squeeze "You don't have to see him ever again if you'd rather not"

"Well," I hesitated. "I never ever want to meet the mean Marc again in my life but... I'm not sure because I don't think he's like that anymore, not after I saw his apology during the memorial service"

There was another long silence before I slowly said "You know, I think it will help if I do meet him again"

"How so?" Erad asked.

"Because" I hesitated to process my own thoughts "I only really remember him as the mean and frightening Reacher commander, if I meet him again and he's not like that anymore then I'll remember him as a nice person"

"I think you're right." he nodded "Well then if you are okay with it, I shall let him know that he can come and visit"

I nodded and took a deep breath "I'm alright with it"

The next few days were a bit strained. I was nervous and on edge whenever the door opened or I heard a vehicle. Erad was worried but I told him I'd be like this until the visit was over.

Finally, the day arrived when Erad said Marc was coming. I was so nervous, and I wasn't exactly sure why, it felt like there could be so many reasons. I hadn't seen him since that day when I'd watched the memorial, but I still vaguely remembered him from the last day on Ithral and the goodbye he'd given at Elitas military port.

I was lost deep in a book when the doorbell rang, and I almost jumped off the couch in fright. Erad stood up from his computer and headed for the door giving me a concerned and unsure look. The next twenty seconds felt so long until finally Erad walked back into the lounge room followed by Marc Huxley.

The atmosphere was a bit more than slightly awkward and a little tense from Erad, who was extremely on edge worrying that I was going to have some form of breakdown or panic attack. I hadn't told him about many details on how Marc had treated me, only slight comments and such. But now, by how nervous he was, I guessed Marc must have told him everything.

I took a deep breath and shook Marc's hand, the contact felt unnerving as I remembered the various kinds I had received from him in the past.

Erad gave an encouraging nod before leaving the room looking very unsure. I knew he was just down the hallway and that at any moment a yell from me would bring him running.

"Hello Winta, I am very glad to see you again, I hope you have recovered well?"

For a few seconds I was too confused at hearing his voice to realise he was talking to me.

"Oh, yes" I tried to pull myself back together "I have recovered mostly, they're just scars now"

He nodded "I'm glad to hear that, I had heard that you were really sick"

"I was," I said slowly feeling extremely embarrassed as I remembered my state during our time together on Ithral "But it was just an infection"

The awkwardness seemed to grow, and I wondered just how I could ever have thought this might be a good idea. Desperate for something to be said I quickly looked back at Marc.

"I ... Erad told me why you wanted to see me again, but you don't have to apologise, there's nothing to apologise for as I've already forgiven you, besides you already apologised at the memorial..." I stopped, shocked at my own speech and felt my cheeks grow hot with a sudden flood of fresh embarrassment.

Marc looked surprised too "Even after everything?"

I nodded, glancing around uncomfortably "Yes, I'm pretty sure I would have been just as horrible if our situations had been swapped"

He laughed half-heartedly "That still doesn't change what I did"

I shrugged "It's all long gone in the past, neither of us are the same person that we were on Ithral, plus we need to move on not go back there..."

He smiled now "You sound very sound and wise, well then, I shall change my goal in coming here to thanking you for forgiving me"

I returned his smile with an effort "You know I have to thank you too, thank you for being so comforting and kind on that last day when..." I paused as I felt my throat tighten and tears come to my eyes.

I felt his hand gently rest on my shoulder and encourage me to sit down on the couch. I took a few deep breaths to calm myself.

He sighed slowly "It was the least I could do after all you had done for me and my people, though I hardly knew myself at the time" his voice sounded far off and thoughtful, he shook himself "Like you said, we need to move on not go back there"

I nodded "I don't want to talk about it, I think both of us know as much as the other, but it's still there"

He shrugged "It's gonna hurt for a long time yet, forever if I know anything about grief, though it does ease with time"

There were a few minutes of silence and to my great relief I could feel the awkwardness had seriously diminished.

"What do you do now?" I said, thinking more out loud than an actual question.

"Well, retirement definitely wasn't for me, just yet" he answered thoughtfully "So I'm currently working for Reacharva's military aid relief as we try to end this civil fighting on the Atravo moons"

Though I had not intended my thought to be answered I was intrigued "Really? That sounds very encouraging, I hope it ends soon"

He nodded "And what do you do?"

I laughed "I'm a cleaner at my parents defence flight training camp"

He smiled "Why'd you laugh? That sounds nice and calm compared to what you used to do"

"It's just so drastically different" I chuckled again.

Suddenly I remembered Erad and jumped up, Marc followed looking concerned.

"What's the matter, are you alright?"

I felt awfully embarrassed again "Yeah, I'm fine, I just remembered that my brother is around and probably really worried"

"True, we better find him, he's a really nice guy"

I nodded turning towards the door as he followed "He is, he's the best brother"

As we wandered around the house looking for Erad we talked of the many things that the future might hold for both of our different lives.

"I want to visit Reacharva one day, maybe when all the civil fighting ends"

Marc grinned "You know Elita is far better?"

"Of course it is" I laughed back "But I still want to see your planet"

"I'll tell you what, I'll contact you as soon as the civil fighting has been resolved, then, if you'd like, I can arrange for you and Erad to come over and visit, maybe we can even organise a meet up with Stan's family?"

I heard the catch in his voice and knew he was worried that mentioning Stan was going to upset me.

"I'd really love that" I answered, mostly composed and even quite happy.

I sensed him relax in relief.

"There's your brother," he said, pointing towards the veranda.

I hurried to the door and Erad rose to catch me in his arms holding me tight.

"Thank you so much," I sighed gratefully.

"You are most welcome," Erad said in relief as he held me close.

A few hours later Erad and I stood side by side as we waved goodbye to Marc while he drove away. I felt like a great heavyweight had vanished from my mind and heart and I let out a deep heartfelt sigh of relief.

"Was it what you needed?" Erad asked as we both headed back inside.

"It was and more, I feel so much more relieved, at ease and peaceful"

Erad smiled in joy "I'm so, so glad"

That night as I watched the stars, I knew I was *fully recovered*. I still missed Stan and sometimes felt much grief over memories but that was okay, and I knew that now more than ever. Those who once had been enemies were now friends, wrongs had been righted and forgiven. The past was in the past and I was happy and willing to leave it there. One day I would visit Reacharva and meet Stan's family and when that day came, I would take it how it came.

With a peaceful sigh I held Stan's badge to my heart. I was not unreasonable in how I felt, I was not weak for feeling what I did, I was not over dramatic for still feeling what I felt, I was not overreacting for having troubles and struggles because of what I had been through.

I was human, I was an honest female who had and felt emotions. What had happened, what I had felt and still did feel was real, I was real.

The End

APPENDIX

PLANETS & PEOPLE INFO

Elita (Elites Home Planet)
•Eradan (Erad) Yovacar 25 – Star-Craft Technician
•Seran Fain 18 – Accountant
Detra: (Elitas Second Moon)
•Mr & Mrs Yovacar – Fighter Pilot Trainers
•Winta Yovacar 20 – Tech Engineer-Strike Pilot

Reacharva (Reacher's Home Planet)
•Marc Huxley 26 – Squadron Commander
•Hank Palace 23 – Squadron Lieutenant
•Stan Whitlock 24 – Tactical Doctor
Atravo: (Reacharva's String of Moons)
•Miss Whitlock 27 – Advanced Tactical Doctor

Ithral: (Ace'tams Home Planet)
Degwa Tribe
•Brega Tadrai 54 - Captain of the Degwa Tribe
•Adreea Tadrai 23 – Degwa Soldier Medic

GLOSSARY

PRONUNCIATION GUIDE

Ace'tam – Ace-tam
Adreea – Ad-ree-ah
Atravo – At-ra-vo
Brega – Bre-ga
Degwa – Deg-wa
Detra – Det-rah
Elita – El-eat-uh
Elite – El-eat
Eradan – Eh-rad-an
Erad – Eh-rad
Fain – Feign
Huxley – Hux-lee
Hank – Hank
Ithral – Ith-rule
Marc – Mark
Palace – Palace
Reacher – Reacher
Reacharva – Reach-arva
Seran – Sir-ran
Stan – Stan
Tadrai – Tad-dray
Winta – Win-tuh
Whitlock – Wit-lock
Yovacar – Yov-a-car

ACRONYM MEANINGS

CEMF: Continuous Electromagnetic Field

CEMP: Continuous Electromagnetic Pulse

EMP: Electromagnetic Pulse

HQ: Head Quarters

PTSD: Post Traumatic Stress Disorder

REFERENCE MEANINGS

Crate Trader: The most easy, simple, and common job in *space trade* throughout the universe.

Elita Claim Code: A set of codes outlining the systems and planets Elita has laid *ownership* claim to.

ABOUT THE AUTHOR

I am an author and artist from Victoria Australia who recently married the love of my life. I love sewing, crafting, gardening, exploring forests and capturing imaginary fantasy worlds in writings, drawings and paintings.

My favourite genre to write in is medieval fantasy closely tied with high fantasy, but I also enjoy writing science fiction, such as this title.

This is the first novel I have completed and published so effectively it is the test one that I am using to learn how to format and publish eBooks, paperbacks, hardcovers and audiobooks.

I plan on this only being the beginning as I have so many more books and stories that I want to finish writing, editing and publishing.